Dumarest stepped closer to where the statue stood. It was, he judged, about twelve times life-sized, the cupped hands some seven feet across. The ball hanging above the cupped palms was about ten feet across and he studied it, frowning, wondering as to its purpose, the markings blotching the shining, metallic surface. A ball poised before her, one she had just tossed upward or was about to catch. Or was it something more than that? The symbolism had to be important. A ball—or was it representative of something special? A world, perhaps?

A world!
Earth!
It had to be Earth!

THE TEMPLE OF TRUTH

E.C. Tubb

DAW Books, Inc.
Donald A. Wollheim, Publisher
1633 Broadway, New York, N.Y. 10019

PUBLISHED BY
THE NEW AMERICAN LIBRARY
OF CANADA LIMITED

DAW Collectors' Book No. 637

DEDICATION

To Glennis McCourt

First Printing, July, 1985

2 3 4 5 6 7 8 9

PRINTED IN CANADA
COVER PRINTED IN U.S.A.

Chapter 1

Karlene shivered. Thirty dozen perlats had been slaughtered to provide her furs yet still she felt the cold. An illusion—born of snow and ice and the pale azure of an empty sky. The visual effects overrode the electronic warmth cossetting her body and she lifted her hands to draw the soft hood closer about her face.

"Cold?" Hagen had noticed the gesture. "Are you cold?"

"No."

"Then—"

"Nothing." An answer too curt and she expanded it as she swept a hand at the vista before them: a landscape of white traced with azure and flecked with motes of nacreous sheen. Out there perspective was distorted so that the mound she looked at could have been a hundred yards distant or a thousand, the dune a thousand or ten.

"There's no warmth," she complained. "No shelter. It's all so bleak. So inhospitable."

He said, "Erkalt is a frigid world, but it has its uses."

"Such as?"

"Low-temperature laboratories. Some mines. Some—" He broke off, knowing she knew the details. "As a site for the games," he said. "As a frame for your beauty. An ice queen should rule over a world of ice."

Empty flattery but she restrained her annoyance. Instead she walked to the edge of a shallow ravine, one barely visible against the featureless expanse. It was empty; a gash cut deep into the snow, pale shadows clustered in its depths. No trace of life yet; looking at it, she felt the familiar touch in her mind.

"Something?" Hagen was beside her, his eyes searching her face. "You catch the scent?" His tone sharpened as she nodded. "When? Soon? Late?"

"Late." The touch had been too gentle. "Sometime ahead but too weak to tell when."

Time and cause—variables beyond her control. Duration weakened impact so that a dire event in the distant future would register as a small incident almost due. An irritation, but one he had no choice but to accept. Now he slipped an arm around her shoulders and led her from the treacherous lip of the ravine.

"Probably a perlat slaughtered for its hide or some other small animal ending its life." He kept his tone light, casual. "Victim of some predator, no doubt. Don't worry about it."

Good advice; to brood on death and fear was to invite madness. Yet, at times, it was hard to ignore the shadows which stretched back through time. In that ravine a creature would die and would know terror before it expired.

"We'll try over to the east," said Hagen. His tone, still light, masked his impatience. "Once we find the right place we can set up the scanners."

"If we find it," she said. "And if it's the right one."

"It will be—you'll see to that."

His assurance held the trace of threat, but she said nothing as he led the way to where the raft stood on the frozen snow. The driver, muffled in cheap furs, touched a control as they climbed aboard, and a transparent canopy rose to enclose the body of the vehicle and protect them from the wind. It droned as they rose, a bitter, keening sound, and she shivered again as the raft moved away from the lowering sun.

"Still cold?" Hagen was concerned. "Perhaps you are ill. I think you should see a doctor when we get back to town."

"No!" Her refusal was sharp. "There's nothing wrong with me. It's just this damned planet."

The snow and ice and shriek of the wind. A sound as if a lost soul was crying its grief as it quested empty spaces. Beneath the raft the ground was a blur of whiteness; a board on which, soon, a bloody game would be played. What did a quarry feel? Fear, that was certain, a rush of terror prior to a savage end, but what else? Hope, perhaps? The belief in the miracle which alone could bring safety? Regret that greed and love of life had led to a frigid hell?

The heaters had taken the chill from the air within the canopy and she loosened the hood, throwing it back from her head and face to release a cascade of hair. It fell in a cloud of shimmering whiteness over the pearly luster of her furs; hair as white as the snow below, as white as the blanched pallor of her skin.

An albino; beneath the silver-tinted contact lenses she wore, her eyes held the pinkness of diffused blood.

"You're beautiful!" Hagen was sincere in his appreciation, eyes studying the aristocratic delicacy of her face; the high cheekbones, the hollow cheeks, the thin flare of nostrils, the curve of lips, the rounded perfection of the chin. Beneath the furs her body was lithe with a rounded slimness. "An ice queen, as I said."

A mutant and hating it despite the wealth it had brought her. Hating the talent she possessed which set her apart, now again making itself manifest within the secret convolutions of her mind.

"Karlene?" Hagen had seen the sudden, betraying tension. "Something?"

"I think so."

"Strong? Close?" He ceased his questioning as she raised a hand. Waited until it lowered. "No?"

"A scent, but it was weak. Where are we?"

Too far to the east and distant from the city. The raft turned as he snapped orders at the driver, slowing as it circled over the too-flat terrain. Hopeless territory for the games as the fool should have known. The vehicle straightened, humps rising in the distance, to become mounded dunes slashed with crevasses torn by the winds, gouged with pits fashioned by storms.

"Anything?" Hagen glanced at the sun as she shook her head. Soon would come the night, the winds, the impossibility of further search. To the driver he said, "Drop lower and head for the north. Cut speed."

"But—"

"Do it!"

Too low and too slow over such broken terrain could lead to disaster; sudden winds, rising from uneven ground, could catch the raft and bring it to destruction. Fears the man kept to himself as he handled the controls.

Waiting, watching, Hagen forced himself to be patient. There was nothing more he could do and his tension could affect the woman's sensitivity. Now Karlene was in command. Until she scented the node, they must turn and drift and turn again in an ever-widening circle. He had chosen the ground, the decision based on skill and experience, but only she could determine the node.

"You've found it?" He had spotted her tension. "The scent?"

She nodded, one hand to her throat, eyes wide at the touch of horror.

"Close?"

"Close." She inhaled, fighting to be calm. "Close and strong. God, how stong!"

The node. The spot where the game would end. Hagen sighed his relief. Now he could relax. The rest was just a matter of routine.

* * *

Leaning back in his chair, Dumarest looked away from his hungry guest. Brad Arken was more like a ferret than a man; thin, sharp-faced, with eyes which quested in continual movement. His clothing was shabby, his skin betraying chronic malnutrition. To feed him was a kindness, but Dumarest was not being charitable.

"Earl?"

"Help yourself. Eat all you want."

The bread, the vegetables, the bowl of succulent stew. He had barely touched them but he had guessed the other's hunger. Could guess, too, at his desperation; the reason he had selected him from those hiring their labor, the reason he had invited him to dine.

Now, as Arken ate, Dumarest looked around. The restaurant was contained within the hotel in which he had a room. Warm light bathed the area enhancing the comfort of soft carpets and heated air. To one side a facsimile fire burned against a wall, the bed of artificial logs glowing red, gold, amber and orange in a framework of black iron.

A glow which merged with the yellow illumination from the lanterns and threw touches of color on the flesh and finery of the others seated at their tables. A crowd, mostly young, all apparently wealthy. They were in an exuberant mood.

"Voyeurs," said Arken. "Here to enjoy the games. Watching in comfort while others do the work. At least they'll keep warm."

His plate was empty, the bowl also. The vegetables were barely touched but the bread had vanished and Dumarest guessed it now reposed beneath the other's blouse. He lifted a hand as Arken wiped his mouth on a napkin. To the waitress who answered his signal he said, "Wine. A flagon of house red."

It arrived with glasses adorned with delicate patterns engraved in the crystal. Dumarest poured, Arken almost snatching up his glass, downing half its contents at a gulp, then, almost defiantly, swallowing the rest.

As he reached for the flagon Dumarest clamped his fingers on the neck.

"Later. First we talk. I'm looking for a man. Maybe you can help me find him. He's old, scarred down one cheek, gray hair and, maybe, a beard." Scant details but all he had. "Celto Loffredo. Once he was a dealer in antiquities."

Arken said, "Erkalt's a big world but sparsely inhabited. The city here, a few installations at the poles. They are staffed by technicians employed by the companies who own them and they're choosy about who they take. An old man, even if indentured, wouldn't be worth his keep. Which brings us back to the city. I guess you've checked the usual sources? Hotels and such?" As Dumarest nodded he continued, "So he isn't living easy and a man without money has little choice. If he's alive he must be on the brink."

"As you are?"

Arken said nothing but the answer was in his eyes and, as he reached again for the wine, Dumarest released his grip on the flagon.

As the man filled his glass Dumarest said,

"This is free but it's all you're going to get. Locate the man I want and it's worth a hundred."

"That isn't enough."

"All I want is a time and place."

"I'll have to check the warrens." Arken was insistent. "Spread the word and ask around. On Erkalt no one does anything free. I'll need cash for expenses, bribes, sweeteners. How badly do you want to find him?" Dumarest didn't answer, and Arken drank and shrugged before drinking again. "All right, so it's your business, but we'd find him quicker if I could put others to work. And it would help if I'd more to go on."

The man was right, but Dumarest had no more to give. A name, a vocation, the hint that the man could have information he wanted. Details gained on another world and a hope followed because he had nothing else.

"How much will you need?"

"For expenses?" Arken didn't hesitate. "A hundred, at least. More if you want to hurry things along. I'll need to hire men to go looking and there are a lot of places Celto could be. But a hundred should do it."

He refilled his glass, looking at Dumarest, hoping he had struck the right note, named the right price. Too little and he would have undervalued himself and lessened the chance of profit. Too high and he could have lost an opportunity. It depended on his host but Arken thought he recognized the type. A man who lived soft and could afford to be generous; the food and wine was proof of that. He dressed plain but that was not uncommon; many tourists tried to seem what they were not. The grey tunic, pants and boots looked new and the knife carried in the right boot could be for effect.

"Well?" The wine had bolstered his courage and Arken pressed his advantage. A man alone, looking for another on a strange world, would need local help. And, if he was in a hurry, he wouldn't want to waste time. "Is it a deal?"

A parasite eager to suck blood—Dumarest recognized the type. Had recognized it from the first and had set the stage to achieve the result he wanted. Arken's greed, channeled and contained, would make him a useful tool.

"Here. A hundred for expenses." Coins rattled on the table beneath his hand then, as Arken reached for them, steel whispered from leather as Dumarest lifted the knife from his boot. In the illumination the blade gleamed with the hue of burnished gold but the needle point resting against Arken's throat held the burning chill of ice. "Rob me and you'll regret it. I want you to believe that."

"I—" Arken swallowed, cringing from the knife, the threat clear in the eyes of the man who faced him. No tourist this, despite his soft living and casual hospitality. No easy gull to be robbed while fed empty lies. "Man! For God's sake! There's no need for this!"

For a moment longer the steel held his eyes, then it vanished as quickly as it had appeared. Arken touched the place where it had rested, stared at the fleck of blood marring his hand. A minor wound, barely noticeable, but the blade could have as easily opened his throat. Wine spilled as Arken tilted the flagon, a small pool of ruby resting on the polished wood of the table. One which looked too much like blood.

He said, unsteadily, "Why do that? We had a deal. You can trust me."

"I'm glad to hear it."

"I'll find him," promised Arken. "If Celto Loffredo is alive I'll find him."

"Tell him nothing when you do. Just bring me word."

Arken nodded, gulping at the wine in his glass, looking at the soft comfort of the room. Those present had seen nothing of what had taken place; Dumarest had masked the incident with arm and body. He remembered the speed, the sting of the point, the naked ferocity he had seen in the eyes and face of his host. There had been no pretence. It had been no empty threat.

"A hundred?"

"Five," said Dumarest. "Less a hundred for each day I'm kept waiting. Keep me waiting too long and I'll want to know why." He touched a finger in the pool of wine and drew a ruby streak over the table. "If you want to quit leave now."

Arken resisted the temptation. His head tilted as Dumarest rose to his feet, yellow light casting a sheen on the smoothness of his clothing. Somber garb but as functional as the man himself.

A hard man who followed a hard road—Arken's hand shook as he reached for more wine.

The restaurant had two doors: one which led through a vestibule to the outside, the other leading into the hotel, the bar, the small casino the place contained. Dumarest heard the click of balls, the chant of a croupier as he fed a spinning wheel.

"Pick your combination. Red, black or one of each. Three chances of winning at every spin of the wheel. Place your bets, now. Place your bets!"

An adaption of an ancient game but one with a false attraction. Winners gained two to one which made the house margin unacceptably high to any knowledgeable gambler. Even so the table was crowded, a matron, her raddled face thick with paint, squealing her pleasure as both balls settled in the red.

"I've won! Jac! I've won!"

Her escort, young, slim, neat in expensive clothing, dutifully smiled his pleasure at her success. Dumarest watched as he helped pile the winnings into a rounded head, two chips vanishing as, deftly, he palmed them from sight. A bonus to add to his fee for the company he provided, the kisses he would give, the caresses she would demand.

"Earl!" The voice was high, clear, rising above the sound of the tables. "Earl Dumarest! Here!"

She was tall, slender, hair neatly cut in a severe style which framed the sharp piquancy of her face. Her smile widened as Dumarest moved toward her. He smiled back; Claire Hashein had once been close.

"Earl, it's good to see you again." Her hand, strong, long-fingered, rested on his arm. "What brings you to Erkalt?"

"What brings you?"

"Business." Her shrug was expressive. "Some

fool of a manufacturer thinks the local furs are unique and insisted that I make a personal selection of the best. Nonsense, of course, any competent furrier could do the job as well as I can, but why should I argue when all expenses are being paid? Anyway, it suits my purpose. You?"

"It suits my purpose also."

"Naturally."

Her hand fell from his arm and she stared up at him, head thrown back a little to expose the long, clean lines of her throat. Now, no longer smiling, she looked older than she had. A skilled and clever woman who wore exuberance like a mask. Then, abruptly, she was smiling again.

"I'm really pleased to meet you, Earl. You came on the *Canedo*?"

The last ship to have landed. "Yes."

"I've been here days. We traveled on the *Gual*. A ghastly journey. The talk was all of the games. I was bored to tears but Carl loved it. He's a natural-born hunter. We met on Servais while I was completing an assignment. Creating a wedding gown for the daughter of the local magnate," she explained. "I guess her recommendation got me my present commission."

She was talking too fast and explaining too much and Dumarest wondered at her confusion. They had met on a journey and parted on landing and the odds were against their ever meeting again. Yet here she was and she was not alone.

"Carl!" She turned as a man thrust his way toward them. As he joined them she said, "Carl Indart—meet Earl Dumarest."

He was tall and broad with close-cropped russet hair, a thin mouth and a pugnacious jaw. His eyes beneath heavy brows were a vivid blue. His ears were small, set close to his skull. He was, Dumarest guessed, younger than the woman and himself. When he smiled he revealed neat, white teeth.

"Earl!" His hands rose, lifting to show empty palms. His grip was warm, friendly, as they closed on Dumarest's own. "Where has Claire been hiding you?"

She said, "Earl is one of the most interesting men I've ever met. You could learn from him, Carl."

"I don't doubt it." The rake of his eyes was the searching glance of a hunter; checking, assessing, evaluating. "I guess you're here for the games. There should be good sport. Are you booked yet?" His eyebrows lifted as Dumarest shook his head. "No? A pity. I've a spot in tomorrow's event. Cost me plenty to get another to yield his place but I figure it's worth it. Maybe I could find another place if you're interested."

"No thanks."

"Don't you like to hunt?"

"It's a chance, Earl," said the woman before Dumarest could answer. "The two of you would make a good team. You'd sweep the board and gain the trophy. It could yield a nice profit."

"We'd break even, at least," urged Carl. "Buying a place won't be cheap and there'd be the hire of gear if you haven't brought your own. But we could make extra on the bets." To Claire he said, "I like the idea. It would add spice to the game. Try and talk Earl into it."

"Why don't you?"

"Bresaw's waiting. He's got the runs from the previous dozen games and thinks there could be a pattern. See you!"

He left with a lift of a hand, brash, arrogant, intent on his own concerns. Dumarest glanced at the woman at his side, saw the shadow on her face, one which vanished as she smiled.

"A boy," she said. "Carl's nothing but a boy at heart. All he can think of now are the games."

"And you?"

"Work. Furs, pelts, hides. Dealers who will try to cheat. Liars who will claim a match where none exists. Well, that's for tomorrow. Now let's have a drink."

The bar was quiet compared to the casino and Dumarest led the way to a secluded table. A waitress came to take his order, returning with tall goblets filled with lavender wine laced with a drifting mist of silver bubbles. Claire snorted as they stung her nose, sipped, laughed her pleasure as her mouth and throat filled with a familiar pungency.

"Earl! You remembered!"

Lavender, lime, some osteth and a touch of chard. The constituents of a drink they had shared in the snug confines of a cabin during a journey which, for her, had ended too soon.

She said, "This is nice but you shouldn't wake old memories. It isn't kind. You know how sentimental I am. Earl—"

"Tell me about Carl."

"What?" She blinked at the abrupt question. "Why talk of him?"

"Why not?" He smiled, masking his interest. "Maybe I'm jealous. How well do you know him?"

"Well enough. He's a hunter. He had some skins for sale and we met, as I told you. I sensed something within him. The strength I'd known in you. It set him apart from the others. God—if you only knew how weak most men are!" She reached for the goblet and drank, almost emptying the container. As she set it down she said, softly, "But Carl isn't you, Earl. He hasn't taken your place. No one could ever do that."

Was she a woman in love—or one acting the part? Dumarest signaled, the waitress bringing fresh goblets filled with the same lavender wine. As she left he smiled at the woman beside him.

"You flatter me."

"I tell the truth. Are you annoyed?"

"Of course not."

"I'm glad." Claire moved closer to him, the long line of her thigh pressing against his own, the touch of her fingers a subtle caress. "You'll never know how much I missed you, darling. Work helped to fill the time and—"

"Carl?"

"To hell with him!" Her voice was harsh, betraying her irritation at the change of subject. "Why talk about him? He doesn't own me."

Dumarest doubted if the man would agree with her. He had radiated a proprietary air and his searching look had been more than a casual examination. Carl Indart, he guessed, could be other than what he seemed. Certainly he was a dangerous man.

Chapter 2

They ran him down at the edge of the foothills close to Ekar's pass and Thorn gloated over his monitors.

"Hell—just look at those peaks! The guy's lost control of his sphincters." His laughter was ugly. "Sure glad that I'm not downwind."

He was a squat, greasily fat man, with mean eyes and a snubbed nose. The twig clamped between his teeth exuded a purple ooze which stained gums and teeth. His furs were worn, stained in places, but he knew his job. Even as Hagen watched, he adjusted the balance on the input; accentuating the terror, the panic and fear. An unnecessary refinement—the quarry faced his end, and those watching would know it. But such attention to detail had made Thorn a top man in his trade.

"Boost visual." Hagen narrowed his eyes as the

screen took on sharper tones. The scanner was floating high and wide but the fisheye lens relayed enough data for the monitor to compensate. "Adjust color."

The scene altered as Thorn obeyed; a subtle shifting of hues which diminished the overriding white and gave greater prominence to the quarry. Crouched between a pair of ice-encrusted rocks, he looked like a ragged doll. One with ripped clothing, dirtied, bruised, broken. Blood showed bright on buttocks and legs. More rested like a badge on his right shoulder.

"That's it." Thorn was matter-of-fact. "They'll get him anytime now. The run's over."

The run but not the end. That would come almost a mile away in the small crevasse Karlene had pinpointed. Already the scanners were in position for wide-angle and close-ups. Others would follow the progress of the hunters. Even now more and more who followed the games would be switching to his channel and paying for the enjoyment of his broadcast. Later there would be tapes, stills, sound recordings of the final moments.

"Move!" Hagen snapped into his radio as the quarry rose unsteadily to his feet. "Close in and seal—you know where."

He had a good team and he relaxed as winking lights on the monitor showed they had swung into action. In twenty or so minutes the quarry would have reached the spot Karlene had noted. The hunters would be close behind. Thirty minutes from now it would all be over.

He had misjudged by five.

"It was crazy!" It was hours later after night

had fallen before he'd had time to join the woman. Now, glasses of sparkling wine in his hands, he relived the moment. "He was dead, down and finished—I'd have offered a hundred-to-one on it. Yet, somehow, he managed to make a final stand." He handed her a glass. "A toast, my dear. To another success!"

"You call it that?"

"What else?" He sensed her mood and became serious. "You aren't responsible for the games, my dear. You merely determine where they will end. There's no cause for guilt in that."

Nor in the furs her talent had brought her. The soft living, the luxury, the comfort she enjoyed. No guilt either in success—Hagen had fought hard to gain what he had. To demean his achievement was to be unfair.

"You're right." She tried to shake off her mood—always she was pensive after a game. "Tell me what happened."

"It was unexpected," he said. "That's what made it so unusual. You know how these things normally end—the hunters close in and it's over. But this time they had to work. The quarry dug himself in and—" He broke off, shaking his head. "Never mind. It's over now. It's all on tape if you're interested."

"Later, perhaps."

Which meant never and he knew it. The thing which others bought and played and gloated over gave her no pleasure. Too often she had felt the touch of death and fear. What for others was a titillation was for her a torment.

He said, abruptly, "Karlene, we've done well

and could do better. I've had offers from the Chi-Hsung Combine. A monopoly on the Vendura Challenge with overlap on the Malik Rites. A three-year contract with bonuses and copyright guarantees. It means less work and more money."

"For me?"

"Of course."

"And you?"

She turned to face the window as he shrugged. Outside the night pressed close despite the triple glazing. Darkness illuminated by starlight which, reflected from the snow, threw a pale, nacreous shine over the landscape. A quiet, peaceful scene, but it wouldn't last. Soon would come the winds filling the air with swirling particles of ice and tearing at the frozen snow. Temperatures would fall even lower than what they were. Predators, now buried deep, would be stimulated by the cold to hunt for prey.

"Karlene?" Hagen was beside her, his face reflected next to her own in the pane. "More wine?"

She had barely touched what she had and she shook her head.

"Then—"

"You drink," she urged. "You have cause to celebrate."

She watched as he turned, noting the movement of his head, the profile of his face as he refilled his glass. A hard face but one which could be gentle. A hard man who could have been her father but who inwardly yearned to become something closer. A partner who wanted to become her lover. Why did she resist him?

"Are you taking the offer?"

"That of the Combine?" He shrugged. "It's a possibility, but there are others. If—"

"Don't let me influence you," she said quickly. "You must do what you want."

"I know what I want." He looked at his glass as if coming to a decision then drank and set it down and came toward her, his face growing large in the window. "Karlene, I have money and I can work. There is no need for you to follow the games here or anywhere else."

"Please!"

"Let me finish." He was stubborn. "You must know how I feel about you. I'm not asking you to love me. I'm just asking you to be with me. Here or on any world you choose. If—" He broke off, looking at her face reflected in the window. "Karlene!"

He turned, catching her as she swayed, recognizing the tension, the strain distorting the lines of her face.

"The scent? But—"

"Here," she gasped. "Close."

"Here? In the hotel?"

She nodded, swallowing, one hand rising to mask the quiver of her lips. Death had warned of its coming and, as always, she wondered if that death were to be her own.

Arken said, "I'm sorry. I've done my best but as yet it hasn't been good enough. The man you want is hard to find."

He stood muffled in a stained and patched thermal cloak, the hood drawn tight, breath forming a white cloud before his face. Dumarest, similarly attired, stood at his side, both men hugging the shelter of an alcove.

He said, "You've spread the word?"

"All over." Arken was bitter. "They take the cash and make the promise and that's as far as it goes. I've run down a dozen leads and all have turned out to be a waste of time. Information I paid for and those giving it swore they had seen Celto Loffredo alive and knew just where he'd be. Liars. Damned liars the lot of them."

Men living on the brink, desperate to survive, willing to say anything for the sake of a night's shelter. Setting immediate food and warmth against the prospect of future punishment. Dumarest understood them as he understood Arken: a man reluctant to admit his failure but more afraid to be thought a cheat.

"I've scanned the streets," he said. "Checked the warrens and now it's down to this." His hand lifted and pointed down the street. "Fodor and Braque. Braque's down the street; two zelgars the night. Fodor charges three. Food included. I'll take Braque."

"No," said Dumarest. "I'll take it. Down the street, you say?"

"To the end then turn left. A green lantern." Arken stamped his feet and glanced at the sky. The stars were dimmed by scudding mist. "Better hurry. The wind's rising."

The wind droned louder as Dumarest made his way down the street, pulling at his cloak, stinging his face with particles of ice. The starlight faded as the air thickened, died to leave a solid darkness broken only by the pale nimbus of high-set lanterns. Light which died in turn as the street filled with a blinding welter of snow.

Dumarest had headed to his left and stood with his hand pressed against the wall. A guide which he followed as he fought the wind. The wall ended and he followed it around the corner tripping as his boot hit something soft. Kneeling, he examined it, finding a body which moved, hearing a thin voice pleading above the wind.

"Help me! For God's sake help me!"

A man, thin, frail, clutched at Dumarest as he helped him to his feet. The wind eased a little and he saw a shapeless bundle of rags, a face half-covered by a cloth, eyebrows crusted with ice.

"Braque?"

"There!" The man lifted an arm. "Don't leave me!"

He clung like a burr as Dumarest moved toward the opening he'd indicated, set beneath a pale, green glow. The light flickered as he approached, vanished as the wind resumed its onslaught. Snow blasted around them as Dumarest forced a passage through heavy curtains. Beyond hung others, a door, a table behind which sat a broad, stocky man.

"Cash." His hand hit the table, palm upward. "Give or go." He grunted as Dumarest fed the hand with coins. "Right. You're in. You?"

The man Dumarest had rescued was old, a ruff of beard showing beneath the protective cloth covering his face. He beat his hands together, shivering, then fumbled at his clothing.

"Where—" His hands moved frantically. "I had

it! I swear I had it! I must have lost it when I fell. Or—" He looked at Dumarest, looked away as their eyes met, thinking better of making an accusation. Instead he tried to plead. "You know me, Sag. I'll pay."

"That's right," agreed the doorkeeper. "And you'll do it now." He frowned at the coin the old man gave him. "Where's the other one?"

"I haven't got it. I'm short, Sag. But I won't eat anything. Just let me stay the night." His voice rose as the man shook his head. "I'll die out there! The wind's blowing hard. For God's sake— you'd kill me for a lousy zeglar?"

For less—Dumarest read the man's intention as he rose from his stool. His hand moved, the coin he held fell, ringing as it hit the floor at the old man's feet. A five zelgar piece.

He said, "Is that what you were looking for?"

"What? I—" Necessity made the old man sharp. "That's it! I knew I had it! Thanks, mister!" He scooped up the coin and slammed it on the table. "Here, Sag, give me my change."

Dumarest looked at the doorkeeper as the old man passed into the shelter.

"Sag? Is that your name?"

"Sagoo Moyna. Why?"

"I'm working for a man who wants to find someone. Celto Loffredo." Dumarest gave what description he had. "If you know where he could be found it could be worth money."

"So I've been told."

"Would he come here?"

"He might. We get all kinds. If he does I'll let

you know. Staying?" He grunted at Dumarest's nod. "Better hurry if you want supper."

It was the swill Dumarest had expected. The shelter, as he'd known it would be, was a box with a low ceiling, poorly illuminated, the air fetid. From the huddled mass of humanity on the floor rose a susurration of groans, snores, ragged breathing, mutters, sighs.

A bad place but outside it would be worse. There the only hope of survival was to find others, make a crude shelter and spend the night huddled together for mutual warmth. A gamble few could win.

Dumarest picked his way through the somnolent bodies and found himself a space. He settled down, fumbling, lifting the knife from his boot and lying with it in his right hand; both hand and blade masked by his cloak. The floor was hard, the smells stronger in the lower air, but the place was warm from the heat of massed bodies and he had known worse.

He relaxed, ignoring the taste of the swill he'd eaten to maintain his pretense, ignoring, too, the odors and susurration around him. Things easy to forget after a time of relative comfort. Beside him a man groaned, turned, one arm moving, the hand falling within inches of Dumarest's face. A gnarled hand, the nails cracked, grimed, the knuckles raw and swollen. A finger was missing, another black from frostbite. As he watched, lice crawled among the thick hairs of the back and wrist.

From somewhere to one side a man screamed.

It was a short, sharp, sound muffled and followed by a blow. Another cursed. Anger at broken rest and a dream which had turned into a nightmare. Dumarest moved a little, closing his eyes, the cloak wrapped tight around his body.

Resting he thought of Claire Hashein.

She had been demanding in her passion; memories and wine inducing a feral desire. His room had become the cabin in which once they had traveled. His bed the stage on which she had enacted a familiar scene. A woman protesting her love, making plans, extracting promises. Demanding more than he was willing to give and offering more than she was able. A game in which he had participated, remembering how wine affected her, how she had talked in her sleep.

Yet, when she had sunken into satiated slumber she had said nothing of value.

Dumarest saw her face as he slipped into a doze. Pleasant features which could be the mask of danger. Had their meeting been truly coincidental? Was she being used without her knowledge?

And what of Carl Indart?

A hard man, ruthless, one with the sadistic streak forming the nature of most who hunted for sport. One who had attached himself to the woman for reasons Dumarest could guess. If the man was hunting him what better way to get close?

He stirred, the prickle of danger warning him as it had so often before. The woman, the hunter, Celto Loffredo whom he had come to find. That man could hold the answer to the question which dominated his life, but had apparently vanished from the face of creation.

Dumarest sighed, sinking deeper into his doze, a montage of faces flickering like the glows of a stroboscope as sleep engulfed him. Men he had known, women he had loved and lost, those who had hated him, those he had been forced to kill.

Fragments of childhood and a life in which the shelter he now occupied would have been the epitome of luxury.

Images which shattered as he woke to the sting of a knife at his throat.

The smells had grown thicker, the mumble of sound new a susurration like the wash of restless waves on a distant shore. The illumination was too weak to throw strong shadows but Dumarest had chosen to rest beneath a light, and on the sleeping body beside him something threw a patch of darkness.

A man, kneeling at his back, stooped, the knife in his hand resting on the hood of the cloak. A slender blade which had thrust through the material to touch the flesh just below the ear. A thief's trick; should he wake and pose a threat the knife would drive home bringing silence and death at the same moment.

"Hurry!" The voice was a whisper. "Get on with it!"

An accomplice; one who would search while the other stood guard. Dumarest lay still as the cloak was moved away from the lower part of his body. Fingers probed at his legs, his boots, the lower edge of his tunic. Places were money could be hidden. He sighed as they reached a pocket.

"Jud?"

"Keep looking."

The man with the knife was a thief not a murderer, reluctant to strike without need. Dumarest built on that advantage. As the fingers delved into a pocket, he grunted, twisted a little, hunched his shoulder, shifting his arm beneath the cloak. Movements which trapped the searching fingers and caused the man to lift the knife from its place. It returned at once to rest lower, the point hard against the collar of Dumarest's tunic.

It thrust as he reared upright, the blade slicing through the plastic to slip harmlessly from the metal mesh buried beneath. Before the man could strike again Dumarest had moved his own knife, the steel shimmering as it swept up and back in a vicious slash, dulling as the edge bit deep.

"God!"

The accomplice cringed as blood fountained from a severed throat, a ruby flood which fell like rain, dying as Dumarest turned, knife stabbing, the point reaching the heart. Blood dripped from the steel as it swung toward the other man. Dumarest recognized the man just as the blade took his life.

"Scum." Sagoo Moyna looked down at the man Dumarest had rescued from the storm. "He sold you out. That's the thanks you get for saving his life."

"The other one?"

"Jud Amnytor. I've had trouble with him be-

fore. Most don't complain when they've been
robbed. Too scared to, I guess. Well, to hell with
them." His foot spurned the dead. "How do you
want to handle this?"

"Quietly."

"That's what I figured. I should report it to the
guards but they must be busy and who wants to
buy trouble? What's it worth for you to stay out
of it?" He blinked at Dumarest's answer. "That
all?"

"Report it and the guards will ask questions.
One might be how Amnytor managed to operate
so long. Another might be why no one's complained. They might think you and he were working together." Dumarest met the other's eyes. "I
might even begin to think you set me up."

"No!" Sagoo glanced at the dead. "It wasn't
like that."

"Then we have a deal?" Dumarest added, as he
looked at his cloak now thick with drying blood,
"Call it the price of a change."

It was dawn when he left the shelter, the wind-
swept streets empty, bleak. Mounds of frozen snow
had piled in corners and hung thick from the
eaves. Brilliant white which hid the dirt and
stains of poverty, the bodies, the debris of the
day. Like a cleansing tide the wind swept clean
the place men had made their own.

As he neared his hotel he heard a man call and
slowed to a halt as Arken ran to join him.

"I'm glad you're early." Arken gasped, beating
his hands as he fought for breath. "This damned
cold tears at the lungs. I tried to wait for you in
the hotel but they wouldn't let me in."

"News?"

He gave it in a small cafe sitting at a table over a mug of steaming tisane. A place catering to those who had finished their term of duty or were about to start work.

"I didn't find the man you want but I met someone who sold me something he owned. A book. I paid fifty for it."

The price Dumarest had paid to dispose of two bodies but, if it was what he hoped, the book was worth a hundred times as much. He took it from Arken's hand. A small, stained volume the covers a dull, mottled green. The pages were brown with age, thick with faded writing. Beneath the cover, printed on an attached insert, he saw the lines and curves of a neat calligraphy.

"Celto Loffredo," said Arken. "That's a book-plate. He put it in to prove the book was his."

Or someone had done it to make that exact point. Arken? It was possible, his time had run out and it was his last hope of earning a reward. Or it could be genuine. Coincidences happened and it would be wrong to be over-suspicious.

Dumarest said, "Is this all? Was there anything else? Clothing," he explained. "Jewelry; rings, bracelets, medallions." Personal items on which figures could have been stamped. Garments which could hold secrets within their seams. "No?"

"Clothing doesn't hang around. It's used, worn, ripped up to make patches. As for the rest—" Arken shrugged and sipped his tisane. "Anything that can buy food or shelter gets sold."

As books got burned but this one had survived. Luck, perhaps. It happened.

Dumarest fingered the volume, wanting to open it, read and examine it, but this was the wrong place and the wrong time. Fatigue would dull the sharpness of his mind and he could miss essential information; a scrap of data which could lead to the answer. He needed to rest, to get rid of the stench of the shelter, the sweat of recent action. The cloak he wore was slimed with dirt and he remembered the lice he had seen.

Arken said, "I'll keep looking if you want. There could be other things, papers, maps, old stuff like the book." He lingered on the word. "Was I right to buy it?"

"Yes."

"Should I buy more if I find them?"

"Not until I've seen what it is. Fifty, you said?"

An inflated price; Arken would be a fool not to have made a profit. His eyes widened as Dumarest thrust coins across the table.

"A hundred! But—"

"This closes our deal. If you find anything new let me know. Here." He dumped the cloak on the table. "A bonus."

"Thanks. It'll pay for some steam. Why don't you join me?"

"No need. I've got my own."

The bath and shower in his room which he yearned to use. The hotel admitted him without hesitation and he climbed the stairs too impatient to wait for the elevator. The corridor was empty aside from a woman busy with a broom who smiled then returned to her duties as he headed for his room. The door swung open to reveal the compartment with its window, furnishings, carpeted floor. The bathroom lay to one side and Dumarest headed toward it, jerking to a halt as he saw the bed.

The bed and the woman sprawled across it. Claire Hashein, naked, lying on her back, arms lifted, legs asprawl, a glint of metal in one hand.

Behind him the cleaner screamed as she saw the blood.

A ruby tide stained the sheets and painted the torso with carmine smears from the gash which marred the throat.

Chapter 3

Prisons held a universal sameness but the one on Erkalt was better than others Dumarest had known. His cell was a box containing a bunk, toilet facilities and nothing else. One wall was made of bars. But there was warmth and light and he was alone. They had taken his clothes and possessions, giving him a pajama-like garb of soft yellow fabric, but had allowed him to retain the book. A selfish act of charity; prisoners who were engrossed did not scream, yell their innocence, shout abuse. Noises Dumarest ignored as, lying on the bunk, he studied what Arken had found.

The book looked old, but age could be simulated. Acids could have browned the pages and faded the ink. Mechanical friction could have fretted the covers. Dyes could have added the stains. Celto Loffredo had dealt in antiquities

and he would have wanted to maintain a supply
of saleable items. If not found they could have
been made.

Would it have been worth his while?

Collectors were willing to pay high for items
they wanted and desire of possession would blind
them to the possibility of forgery. Even on Erkalt
such collectors could be found. Would a man,
cold, hungry, living on the brink, have hung on
to something of worth?

Or had the book meant more to its owner than
the comfort its sale could have provided?

The pages made small whisperings as Dumarest
turned them, frowning as he tried to decipher the
crabbed, faded script. A journal, he guessed. A
diary relating the important events of a man's
life. A trader; many pages bore figures which
could have been a record of profits and losses.

On one page, soiled by a stain which could
have been caused by water or wine, he read barely
discernible words.

> ". . . loaded three bales of ossum . . . will
> try and get . . . passage on the *Gillaus* to . . .
> Blackheart ill and I sat with him. Fever, I
> think; he rambled on about. . . . Crazy but
> some of it made an odd kind of sense. Will
> try. . . . If true then. . . ."

The light was too poor, the writing too faded
for Dumarest to make out more. He turned the
pages, tried to read another, his eyes moving
over a column of figures, the last heavily under-

lined. As he frowned at it the bars rattled, the door sliding open beneath the hand of a guard.

"A visitor," he said. "Your advocate."

Shanti Vellani was small, neat, his face sharp, his eyes like those of a bird. Clear, brown, always on the move. He remained silent until the guard had locked him within the cell and had moved away.

"You're looking well, Earl. I'm pleased to see it. There's no sense in anyone beating their head against a wall."

"You've news?"

"Of course, but first a small matter of business." Vellani took a slip of paper from an inside pocket. "Your account to date. It includes expenses. If you'd like to authorize payment?"

Dumarest took it and studied the amount. It was high but the best did not come cheap and he needed the best. He rolled the ball of his thumb over the sensitized portion.

Handing it back he said, dryly, "I take it the news is bad."

"It could be better." Vellani tucked the slip into his pocket then sat down beside Dumarest on the bunk. "I'll be frank with you. On the basis of available evidence you haven't a chance. The prosecution has a watertight case."

"I didn't kill her."

"So you say." Vellani lifted a hand as if to still any protest. "But look at it from the other side. You and the victim were lovers. She was close to another, Carl Indart, and you could have wanted her to break with him. She refused, you lost your temper, there was a brief struggle and—" His shrug was expressive.

"That's assumption, not proof."

"The cleaner saw you enter the room."

"Which is proof that I wasn't in it. Hell, I wasn't even in the hotel that night. I told you that."

"Your alibi." Vellani pursed his lips. "As regards the hotel you could have left it anytime after killing the woman. All the porter can swear to is that you demanded entry shortly after dawn."

"So?"

"Claire Hashein was killed approximately three hours before sunrise. You could have sneaked out just before dawn and returned to establish your innocence. I merely relate the possibility."

"I've a witness."

"Brad Arken. All he can swear to is that he met you close to the hotel that morning."

"We met the previous night."

"And parted." Vellani shook his head. "It would have been easy for you to have returned to the hotel after leaving him. The public rooms were still open and, in the crowd, you wouldn't have been noticed. Then to your room, the rendezvous with the victim, the argument, the act, the attempt to establish your absence. It's speculation, true, and I could argue it out of court, but there's more. The report made by the examining investigator, for example. The victim was lying supine on the bed. She was naked. Her hands and arms were upraised. Bruises were found on her cheeks as if she'd been slapped. The fingers of the right

hand clutched a key which fitted the lock of your
room."

"I didn't give it to her."

"Can you suggest how she got it?"

"Borrowed a spare from the desk. Had a copy
made—your guess is as good as mine." Dumarest
added, bitterly, "Does it matter? The key didn't
kill her."

But it may have led to her death. Dumarest
imagined the scene, Claire, in love, wanting to
surprise him. Entering his room, stripping, bath-
ing, lying on the bed waiting for him to join her.
Not knowing he was absent from the hotel. Falling asleep, perhaps, to wake and meet her death.

Who would have wanted to kill her?

Why?

Vellani said, "The collar of your tunic was
scarred as if by a metal instrument. It could have
been the key."

"It could have been many things. Assumption
isn't evidence."

"Medical testimony is. The bed was soaked with
blood. It must have sprayed from the severed
arteries of her throat and traces were found on
the carpet and far walls. The medical conclusion
is that such a violent and sudden release of blood
would have given the murderer no chance to
have escaped contact." Pausing, the advocate
added, "Tests revealed flecks of blood on your
clothing. They are of the same group as the victim's. More blood was found on your knife and, it
too, belongs to the same group. As far as the
prosecution is concerned that's all they need."

Motive, means and opportunity—and the damning evidence of the blood. A coincidence; the blood spraying from the thief he had killed had been of the same group as Claire's.

Dumarest said, "If the murderer was stained he'd have to have washed off the blood. Were traces found in the bathroom?"

"Yes. Smears around the edge of the shower drainpipe." Vellani added, "It doesn't help. You— he—could have washed down but missed the traces later found."

"My alibi?"

"It doesn't stand up. Sagoo Moyna denies he's ever seen you."

"He's lying!" Dumarest looked down at his hand where it rested on his knee. It was doubled into a fist. Deliberately he forced himself to relax. As the hand opened he said, "Others must have seen me. There was a man serving the food, and plenty used the shelter that night. They couldn't all have been asleep."

"They weren't."

"Then—"

"Listen to me, Earl, and follow what I say." Vellani edged a little closer, his voice lowering as if he were afraid of being overheard. "I'm not a fool. Scum like Sagoo Moyna will lie for the sake of it but he had a reason. I sent men to find out what it was. You killed that night. I'm not arguing how or why but it happened. Two men dead and Sagoo was paid by you to dispose of them. Do you honestly believe he's going to stand up in court and admit to that?"

"As long as he admits I was there."

"It's too late for that. The prosecution will want

to know why he's changed his story. They'll probe, use devices to check his veracity. Use them on you, too, once they are introduced. The truth will come out—but will it do you any good?"

He had killed an armed thief who had tried to rob him. Self-defense and so justified on the majority of worlds. Even on Erkalt where to kill was to commit the most heinous of crimes. But the other one? The old man?

Dumarest had struck out in unthinking reflex, killing before he had seen the face, recognized a deadly threat. To have delayed could have cost him his life—an assumption he was not permitted to make.

"You're in a bind," said Vellani. "If I get you off one hook you'll be stuck on another and the end will be the same. Twenty years' slave-bondage—need I tell you what that means?"

Locked in a collar which could tear at his nerves or blow off his head at the whim of the controller. One which would detonate if he tried to break it free. A life of helpless obedience.

"You'd be sold to a low-temperature laboratory," said the advocate. "If you manage to serve your time you'll be the first. The record is five years." Pausing Vellani added, "I've spoken to the prosecutor. He's willing to give you an out."

"Such as?"

"You can volunteer for quarry."

The games had started as fun, developed into a sport and were now a bloody slaughter. An attraction which brought tourists flocking to Erkalt during the season. Their money stimulated the economy and fed the parasites that fattened on the ritual; people like Meister and Travante who supplied gear for the hunters; Yegorovich and Mickhailovich who dealt in miniatures, souvenirs, mementoes of the ritual; Pincho and Barrass and Valence with their tapes and stills and tips as to where the quarry could be found.

Entrepreneurs like Hagen.

Murderers like herself.

Karlene moved through the crowd like a silver ghost, tall, impassive, acknowledging greeting with a twitch of her lips, a gesture of a hand. Always it was like this before a hunt; the crowd gathered to discuss the prospects, assess chances, probable routes, odds, the time the quarry would be able to remain free, the moment when he would be run down and his blood sent to stain the snow.

But, more than the rest, they had come to see the man himself.

"Hard." She heard the comment as she passed a man talking to a companion. "I know the type. A killer, too, from what I hear. He'll make a run for it. It'll be good sport. You in for a place?"

"Who isn't?"

The initial raffle. A score would win and be charged extra for the privilege of taking part. Half their fees would be placed within the trophy; the prize for the hunter who won. Given to the quarry together with his freedom should he be lucky enough to make it. Some had gone free—a few spread over the years; enough to maintain the conviction that the quarry had a chance, though that was almost eradicated now by her talent.

"Karlene!"

Hagen waved to her from where he stood with a bunch of others. Hunters from their clothing and interest. She waved back, expecting him to join her, but he was too engrossed in conversation. Business, she guessed, he rarely wasted a moment in his determination to be the best. Alone she moved on to where a wide pane of clear glass almost filled one wall.

Behind it was the quarry.

She had seen them before, Hagen insisting, thinking it helped to refine her talent. Men who stood and looked defiantly at those who had come to gape. Others who paced like restless beasts; nerves too tense to rest. Some had huddled in corners defeated before they had even begun.

Dumarest sat, apparently asleep.

The chair was large, ornate, bolted to the floor so as to face the window. Its arms and high back were covered with scarlet fabric, emphasizing the plain neutrality of his garb. A book, closed, lay on his lap, held by the weight of one hand. His head was supported by the high back of the chair, his face like a mask carved from stone.

Hard, the man had said, and she could see why. The face, the shape of the body, the hand on the book—all gave the impression of strength. Then she realized that he wasn't asleep at all but merely resting. A man conserving his energy, waiting, wrapping himself in a web of isolation. A disappointment to those who had come to stare.

"A killer!" The woman at her side hissed to her

companion, voice low as if afraid the quarry would hear. "He was charged with murder—I had it from a friend in the prosecutor's office. A woman. His mistress. He cut her throat."

"There was doubt."

"But—"

"The evidence was against him, true, but still there was doubt." The man was emphatic. "That's why he was given the chance to volunteer for quarry."

"He could escape!"

"I doubt it. A score of the best will be after him. Nitscke, Sparkissian, Ivanova—Indart has offered ten thousand for a place should he lose out on the draw. You're looking at a dead man, my dear. He hasn't a chance."

That prophecy she would help make come true.

Karlene stepped closer to the glass, curious as to the book, the reason why he should have chosen to read. A religious work of some kind, she guessed, one filled with messages of comfort. As her hand touched the pane Dumarest opened his eyes. Looking at her, he smiled.

"Karlene?" It was Hagen finally coming to join her. "Are you ready?"

She ignored him, looking at Dumarest. He was no longer smiling but the expression had been unmistakable. Almost as if he had recognized an old friend and had smiled a greeting and then, too late, had recognized his error. But his eyes remained fastened on her and, as he straightened in the chair, the book fell from his lap. Small, old, mottled—if it had a title she couldn't see it.

To Hagen she said, "The woman who was killed—describe her."

"What?" He blinked at the question then obeyed. "Why?"

"Nothing." Their appearances were totally dissimilar so he could not have imagined he was seeing a ghost. Someone else, perhaps? "Tell me how she died."

She frowned as she listened, looking at Dumarest, understanding why there should have been doubt. A brutal act of savage, uncontrollable rage—but the man ·who was supposed to have done it simply wasn't the type. No one governed by such emotions could have sat calmly reading while death was so close.

Did he realize there was no escape?

That the chance was a gamble? An adventurer certainly; one who had long learned to rely on no one but himself. A man who now had no choice but to play the murderous game others had devised.

"Karlene?" Hagen was growing impatient. "We're behind time, my dear and—" He broke off as a man thrust his way toward them. A hunter and one with a question. "Not now!" Hagen cut him short at the first word.

"But—"

"Later." To Karlene he snapped, "We've a lot to do and not much time to do it in. The raft's waiting. Let's go."

A summons she reluctantly obeyed, lingering, hoping Dumarest would smile again, wishing she were the person for whom he smiled.

*   *   *

Small things were important if he hoped to survive. With Loffredo's book safely tucked in a pocket of his tunic Dumarest concentrated on the meal before him. It was a good one: meat, wine, rich bread, nourishing pastes. He ate well, his guard nodding approval.

"Good. You've got sense. A quarry needs all the energy he can get. I know. I've been out there."

"As quarry?"

"A hunter. A real one. I was after pelts and they don't come easy. Finally I went too far and stayed too long. When I got back they took off most of a leg." The guard slammed his hand against the prosthesis he wore. "The cold," he explained. "Frostbite and gangrene. It finished me as a hunter and I was lucky to be taken on as a guard."

Dumarest said, "Tell me about the others. Quarries, I mean."

"Fools, most of them. They picked at their food as if it would poison them. Some spent half the night praying when they should have been getting their rest. A waste—if they hoped for a miracle they didn't get it. Some used their heads and a few even managed to make it. Not many and not recently, but it can be done."

"How?"

"Luck. Skill. Hell, if I knew for certain I'd volunteer myself." The guard looked at the table, the remains of the meal. The wine was untouched. "Finished?"

"I've had all I want." Dumarest gestured at the wine. "It's yours if you can use it."

"Well—"

"Go ahead. Drink to my success." He waited until the guard had obliged. "Can you tell me anything about what's out there?"

His public ordeal was over. Now, at midnight, he had been fed and a cell waited to hold him while he slept. The guard would stay in the room in which he had eaten. One man to keep watch, but there would be others close by. Even if he broke free there was nowhere to go.

Relaxing, Dumarest listened as the man explained what he had to face. Snow, ice, winds which changed the terrain and made maps useless aside from permanent landmarks. Gullies which formed twisting mazes; blind alleys, open spaces devoid of cover. And the cold—always the cold.

"You'll want to rest," warned the guard. "Don't. If you do you'll find it hard to get going again. You'll slip into a doze and when the hunters find you you'll be dead. Keep moving and stay alert." He finished the wine, burped, looked at the empty glass. "I hope you make it."

"So do I."

"You'll get an hour's start before the hunters are loosed and anything goes. Killing is allowed. All you've got to do is to reach home before they catch you."

Home: one of two points, each spelling safety. Get to one and the rewards would be his.

"Money and freedom," said the guard. "And more." His wink was expressive. "You could be in for a nice surprise."

The choice of women eager to try a new experience. Those who would have added their names to the rest. Money too in return for his attentions. Harpies common to the arena, stimulated by the sight of blood and combat—the spectacle of pain and death.

Dumarest said, dryly, "You have to pluck the fruit before you can eat it."

"True, but it's nice to know it's there."

"I'm more interested in you having worked as a hunter." Dumarest was casual. "I've done some hunting myself but never in the conditions you've got here. I guess it's hard to make a living."

"You can say that again." The guard slapped at his artificial leg. "Too damned hard at times. But it can be done. Sometimes you can get a few really good pelts and cash in."

"If you know how," agreed Dumarest. "But how do you learn? Were you taught or did you do it the hard way?"

These questions supplied details and led to others in turn. It wasn't hard to guide the conversation. The guard was eager to talk, pleased at the chance to display his knowledge and gratified at Dumarest's unfeigned interest. It was two hours later when, yawning, he suggested that it was time to sleep.

Locked in his cell, lying supine on the bunk, Dumarest stared up at the ceiling. Reflected light from the other room cast a pearly shimmer on the unbroken surface. A screen on which to cast mental images and he reviewed what he had learned from the guard; the shape of native predators, their habits, their ferocity. An hour after dawn he would be thrown among them.

The shimmer blurred a little as he began to drift into sleep, the mental images fading, merging to blend into a new pattern. One of a face and a cascade of silver hair, skin with a pallor emulating snow. A woman who had reminded him of another now long gone in space and time.

Had she bet on his success?

Would she be watching as the hunters came after him to take his life?

Chapter 4

It promised to be a good day. Later there might be a little wind but now everything was clear, cold, crisp and hard. From her seat in the raft Karlene could see the empty spaces below, the small huddle of men around the hut at the starting point. This time it was close to Elman's Sink, an expanse of rough, undulating terrain. In it a quarry could founder and lose his lead.

"I wish they'd hurry." A woman beside her was petulant in her complaint. "The hour must be up by now."

"Another five minutes." Her companion, a middle-aged man, glanced at his watch. "Look! One of them is impatient!"

A man had broken from the huddle to stride over the snow. A marshal ran after him, signaled for him to return. After some delay the man obeyed.

"Indart," said the woman. "I bet that was Indart. He has a special interest. Well, it shows the marshal's are fair."

And she would think the games were fair. Many would agree with her. A man, running, given a start. Others following, picking up his trail, chasing him as he headed for safety. All would be protected against the cold. All equally armed.

But the quarry would have no electronic heat warming his body, no food, no stimulants, no drugs. He would be wearing eye-catching brown and be plunging into the unknown. One against twenty—how could he hope to survive?

Karlene closed her eyes, seeing again the man in the chair, his opened eyes, his sudden smile. Something had touched her then as it never had before. The feeling had ridden with her in the raft as she had hunted for scent.

Which had made her do what she had done.

"Now!"

The shout jerked open her eyes as, below, the hunters streamed after their quarry. A score of running figures, some too eager, others, more experienced, holding back in this, the initial stage. They scattered as she watched; human dogs searching for the trail, questing over the frozen snow.

"That's it." The woman next to Karlene sighed her disappointment. "I'd hoped to see the quarry. Sometimes you can but this one's out of sight. Why can't they let us follow the games from the air?"

A matter of policy; rafts would follow the quarry

and the hunters would follow the rafts to make an easy kill. It was better to ban the rafts and force those interested to pay for the use of broadcast-action. Even so the skies wouldn't be clear. Scanners would be riding high and they would be thick at certain areas.

Karlene could do nothing about that and she forced herself to relax as the raft headed back toward the city. She had done all she could—the rest was up to the quarry.

Dumarest was in hiding.

He crouched in deep snow; a small cave gouged from the side of a mound, sheltered him from viewers above. He wore rough clothing topped with thermal garments which enfolded his body, legs, feet and head in a thick, quilted material. Gloves protected his hands. He had not been allowed to retain his knife but had been given a spear; a five-foot shaft of wood tipped with a foot of edged and pointed steel.

A weapon which could be used as a probe, a balance, a staff, it emulated the natural weapons of a beast of prey. With it he could kill if faced by a hunter.

It lay beside him as he crouched in the snow, the blade showing him the position of the sun. It was rising in the east; the shrunken ball of a white dwarf star, radiating light but little heat. In three hours it would be at zenith; in eight, night would close over the land. A freezing, bitter darkness which would last for six hours. If a quarry failed to reach a point of safety before then he was reckoned to be dead.

Dumarest moved a little, feeling the numbing

bite of the cold. He had rested too long, but to
run without a plan of action was to invite certain
death. To run east or west? A "home" lay in each
direction. If he ran east the rising sun would
dazzle the eyes of his pursuers but not for long
enough. To run west would be to reveal his dun-
colored clothing against the snow. He looked at
it, knowing what he had to do. The risk he had to
take.

Waiting, he looked at the blade of his spear.

Albrecht was enjoying himself. His first visit
to Erkalt and he was thrilling to the game. Luck
had drawn him a hunter's place and he tingled to
the crispness of the air, the physical exertion
which sent blood rushing through heart and brain.
He had hunted before and knew how a quarry
would act. He would run and keep on running,
heading directly for safety, driven by panic and
fear as were all hunted things. Bursting his lungs
to gain speed and distance then, when exhausted,
to sink in a quivering heap to wait final dispatch. Beast or man it was all the same—his real
opponents were his fellow hunters.

He looked at them where they had scattered.
Algat far to his right with three others with him;
they would probably have agreed to work as a
team and to share the trophy. To his left Lochner,
tall, determined, raced ahead as if speed alone
would give him victory. Others. Indart among
them, trailing a little as if satisfied to let others
do the work of eliminating false trails and deceptive starts. Cunning, men waiting to isolate the

true line of flight, conserving their energy for a time of greater need.

A crevasse opened before him and he jumped it, holding his spear high. Another, too wide to jump, into which he descended, following traces which could have been made by running feet. Following it he dropped below the surface and out of sight of any watchers. A white, fur-clad figure almost invisible against the snow.

One which threw a shadow on polished steel.

Dumarest watched as it grew, turning the blade so as to avoid betraying reflections, tensing as the sound of footsteps came close. A soft padding which made it hard to determine true distance. Hard to decide whether or not the man was alone.

A gamble; one man he could take, two he could handle, more and he would be the target of killing spears. A risk he had to take.

Dumarest rose as the footsteps neared the hide. Snow showered from his head and shoulders as he straightened, lunging forward, the butt end of the spear slamming at the head of the figure before him. A blow softened by the thick fur of the hood and Albrecht staggered back, his own spear lifting in defense—but was knocked aside as Dumarest struck again, the blunt end of the shaft driving beneath the hood and impacting the temple.

As the hunter fell, Dumarest looked around, spear at the ready, eyes narrowed as he searched the crevasse, the snow and ice to either side.

Nothing, but speed was essential. He pulled at the fallen man's garments, tearing free the furs and the wide belt holding fat pouches. Stripping

off his own thermal garments he donned the furs.
The belt followed and he paused, listening, eyes
again searching the area. Only then did he dress
the unconscious man in his discarded clothing.

Karlene said, firmly, "It was an act of mercy.
"He could have left Albrecht to die."

"He did." Hagen was burning with excitement.
"Why can't you see that?"

"He could have killed the man."

"Speared him, yes," admitted Hagen. "But that
would have soiled the furs with blood. Instead he
chose to stun—have you ever seen a man move
so fast? I barely saw the blow and the hunter
couldn't have stood a chance. Dumarest wanted
his furs and supplies and, by God, he got them."

And had left the hunter dressed in a quarry's
garb. Only luck had saved him—the hunter running in for the kill had recognized him almost
too late. The thrust of his spear, barely diverted,
had caught him in the shoulder instead of the
chest.

"A decoy," said Hagen. "The attack served a
double purpose; while hunting the decoy they
allowed him time to escape." He frowned at his
maps, his monitors. "Which?" he murmured. "East
or West? Are you sure about the node?"

"You know what I told you."

But not all she knew—suspicion, lying dor-
mant, had suddenly flowered after she had seen
Dumarest in his prison. Small things: men too
eager to talk, hunters intent on private conversation, expressions she recognized from those more
keen on winning bets than following a sport.

Inside information—had Hagen found a way to add to his income? Bets as to the result, the time and place? Tips to the hunters as to where the quarry would meet his end?

Suspicions which had caused her to be reticent. She said, "What happens now?"

"Nothing. The game goes on."

"With Dumarest dressed the way he is?"

"There's nothing against it in the rules." Hagen was patient. "Now the hunters know what's happened they can guard against it. Work in groups," he explained. "Stay close together and ready. All Dumarest has gained is a little time."

The time factor diminished as he lunged through snow and over ice. The furs helped, but he had been unable to take the electronically heated undergarment Albrecht had worn and the cold was an almost tangible enemy. It numbed feet and hands, clawed at his face, sucked at his energy. Stumbling, he fell, rolled down a slope, rose to his feet to stagger on. Behind him the betraying traces he had left showed like gashes on the smooth landscape.

As every footstep he took showed the path of his progress.

Only the wind could cover his trail and, with the wind, would come the blizzards, the freezing chill of incipient night.

And the hunters were close.

"There!" Indart pointed with his spear at the straggling line of footsteps. "Some of you follow. I'll cut ahead to wait before Easthome." He snarled

at an objection. "To hell with the trophy—I want
the man!"

He lunged ahead before any could argue, four
at his heels, following a man they could trust.
Others, less influenced, moved on their own paths,
some toward the other point of safety, the rest
following the trail. If they could move no faster
than Dumarest they would never catch him but
it was easier to follow a path than to make one.
Given time they would spot the hurrying figure.
None had any doubt as to what would happen
when they did.

Dumarest shared their conviction.

He had halted to examine the contents of the
pouches, eating the food he found there, taking
some of the stimulants they contained. The place
he was heading for was marked by a beacon but
first he had to get close enough to spot it. The
sun was now well past zenith and the snow crack-
led beneath his feet. Clouds now flecked the sky
and he studied them as he checked time and
distance. Already the hunt had lasted longer than
usual; he had deliberately taken a winding route.

Now he turned and moved in a direct line
along the path of a gulley, rising to slip into a
crater-like pit, rising again to lope along a ridge.

His movement was spotted and he heard the
yell behind him as he raced on, exertion making
him dangerously warm. Sweat would soak his
clothing, would freeze, would cover him with a
film of ice. Yet to delay would be to take too big a
gamble.

Above him, floating high, drifted the eyes of
watching scanners.

He ignored them, watching the sky, the gathering cloud. The sun grew darker, shadows thick over the azure-tinted snow. Dark patches into which his own shadow merged and blurred and, suddenly, disappeared.

"Gone!" Hagen shook his head. "Thorn? Any sign?"

"None."

"What is it?" Karlene had insisted on joining Hagen at the monitors. "What's happened?"

"Dumarest's vanished. At least we can't spot him. Damn!" The hunters were close, coming in for the kill, but without a quarry they would look stupid. As would his broadcast. "Thorn? Get in close. Use infra-red. We've got to locate him."

"No!" Karlene shouted her objection. "That isn't our job. Do it and I'll report you!"

"Damn you, woman, I'll—" He saw her face, read her determination. Swallowing his anger he said, mildly, "We need it for the broadcast. It'll make no difference to the game but it makes a hell of a difference to the entertainment value of what we put out. Surely you can see that?"

"Do it and this is the last time we work together. I mean that!"

A threat he recognized. Turning to the monitors he said, "All right, Thorn. Leave it for now. Concentrate on the node."

Dumarest had gone to ground, burrowing into the snow, kicking it after him so as to block the entrance to the passage he was now making. Inching forward with twisting wriggles of his body, compacting the snow around him as if he

had been a worm. Moving silently, invisibly as
the guard had told him hunters on Erkalt had to
do to reach a nest of perlats. The cold was a
burning shroud around his body, the air limited
so that his lungs panted for oxygen, the exertion
sapping his reserves, but he kept on, the spear
dragging behind him.

Halting he moved it forward, thrust it ahead,
used it as a probe. It touched something hard and
he moved to one side. A boulder, a long-buried
mass of rock or a somnolent predator—all things
he wanted to avoid. Instinct guided his direction;
a wavering half-circle which should take him
back far from where he had dived into the snow.
Behind it and the hunters who even now could be
probing at it with their spears.

He saw them as he cautiously thrust his head
through the snow. A tight cluster with others
standing closer to him, all looking at the place
where he had entered the mound.

"Anything?" One called out to those busy with
their spears. "Did you get the swine?"

"Don't kill him if you find him," said another.
"Let's make him pay for what he did to Albrecht."

"Indart wants him."

"Too bad. He should be here." A figure thrust
his spear into the snow. One humped and monstrous in his furs. Wind caught and lifted the
crest of his hood. "Come on the rest of you. Let's
dig him out."

The wind gusted as Dumarest eased himself
from the mound. Rising he blended with the background, white, furred, indistinguishable from the

others. Thrusting with his spear, trampling the snow, he masked the signs of his egress.

"Gone!" The big hunter snarled his anger. "He's gone!"

"How?" Another straightened and looked around. "If he's not here then where is he?"

A question answered as soon as someone thought to count heads. Dumarest moved forward, stabbing at the snow, probing to find the mass he had avoided. Rock or stone would be of no help but the luck which seemed to have deserted him could have returned.

"Here!" He called out, voice muffled, one arm waving. "There's something down here!"

He moved aside as others came to probe with their spears. One grunted as his tip found something more solid than frozen snow. Grunted again as he thrust harder, the grunt turning into a shout as, beneath him, the snow erupted in a burst of savage fury.

A beast half as large again as a man. One with thick, matted fur covering inches of fat. The limbs were clawed, the jaw filled with savage teeth, the short tail tipped with spines. A predator woken from somnolence by the prick of spears. Enraged and seeking blood.

A hunter screamed as closing jaws shattered the bone of his leg. Screamed again as the tail dashed the brains from his splintered skull. Another, foolishly courageous, tried to fight. A paw knocked the spear from his hand, returned to tear the hood from his head, the flesh from his face. Blinded, shrieking, he died as a blow snapped his spine.

The rest began to run, two falling beneath the predator, another stumbling to sprawl on the ground as Dumarest thrust the shaft of his spear between his legs. Bait for the beast should it come after him; one opponent the less to worry about if it did not.

The wind rose a little as he raced on, stinging particles filling the air, blinding, confusing his sense of direction. In the distance he could hear shouts as a hunter tried to gather the rest to form a mutual protection. He moved away from the sound, halted, waited until the wind fell and the air grew clearer. The sun was low now and he moved on, away from it, relaxing as, far ahead, he saw a winking glow.

The light of the beacon which spelled safety.

Men rose from the snow as he neared the hut on which the beacon was mounted.

He slowed as he saw them; hunters lying in wait, now closing in for the kill. Three of them and there could be more. His back prickled to the warning of danger and he guessed others were behind him.

Blood spilled by the awakened predator had stained his furs and Dumarest staggered, limping, a man wounded and in pain. He halted as the others came close, one hand lifting to gesture at his rear.

"A beast," he gasped. "It came out of the snow. Killed the quarry and got two others. We scattered. I was hurt but—"

"Your name?"

"Ellman." Dumarest muffled the sound but knew better than to hesitate. "Brek Ellman."

A gamble—one he lost.

"Liar!" The hunter lifted his spear. "He sold his place to me!"

Dumarest dropped, the thrown spear lancing above his head, turning, rising to meet a furred shape rushing at him from his rear. Wood made a harsh, cracking noise as he parried the other's thrust, his own blade darting forward to penetrate the open hood, the flesh beneath. As the man fell, screaming and clutching at his face, Dumarest snatched up the fallen spear, hurled it at another hunter, followed it with a savage lunge. One which penetrated fur, hit metal, the point glancing upward. Dumarest continued the motion, coming close, feeling the cold burn of steel as a blade gashed his side.

As the man tried to strike again Dumarest ripped the hood from his face, jerked free his spear, sent the blade deep into the throat.

As carmine gushed to fill the air with a ruby rain he turned to face the rest.

Three of them, two closer than they were before. One had thrown his spear and now, weaponless, backed away. He would try to rearm himself but, for the moment, could be ignored. The others meant to kill.

Dumarest acted while they were still cautiously advancing. The wound in his side was leaking blood and the cold was a mortal enemy. To wait too long was to waste his strength and he had none to spare. He stooped, snatched up the dead man's spear, ran forward with one in each hand.

The hunter nearest to him backed, holding up his weapon. A man afraid; quarry should be helpless, cringing, easy to kill. A hunter's sacrifice dispatched at a safe distance with bullet or laser-burn. Now he faced a man, hurt, stained with blood, armed as well as himself, intent on taking his life. Too late he realized that he had to fight to save it. Fight and win. He decided to run and died as steel found his heart.

As the unarmed man died as Dumarest threw his other spear; receiving the same mercy as he would have given.

"Fast." Carl Indart threw back his hood. "Fast but a fool. You've disarmed yourself."

He stepped closer, feeling safe against an un-armed man, his face ugly with a gloating satis-faction. A man confident of victory. One who felt the need to talk.

"You're good," he said. "I knew it from the first. What you did to Albrecht proved it. But, as good as you are, I'm better. This proves it." He lifted his spear. "Steel against flesh—what odds would you give on your survival?"

Dumarest said, "You killed Claire Hashein. Why?"

"Does it matter?"

"To me, yes. Was it orders or—"

"No one gives me orders!" Rage flashed like a storm over Indart's face. "No one!"

"Who sent you after me? The Cyclan?" Dumarest read the answer in the shift of the other's eyes. "You fool. Didn't they tell you they wanted me alive?"

Talk to distract as he eased forward. Words which stung and diverted the hunter's attention. Made him forget the speed on which he had commented. Even so, native caution made him wary. Steel shimmered as he moved the spear in his hands.

Shimmered and flashed as Dumarest lunged.

He felt the kiss of it as it brushed his cheek, the burn as it sliced through fur to hit his shoulder then the shaft was in his hand, the fingers of his other stiffened, stabbing at Indart's throat, hitting the chin as the hunter lowered his head. A wasted blow, followed by another to the eyes, hitting the brows, the heel of the palm following to smash against the temple.

As Indart fell Dumarest jerked the spear from his hand, twisted it, thrust the tip of the blade beneath his chin as together they hit the snow.

"Talk, you bastard! Talk!"

"Go to hell!"

Indart was stubborn to the last. Lifting his hands, his arms to rest above his head, writhing as the steel drove into his throat. Dying as the woman had died—but slowly, slowly.

Chapter 5

Hagen stormed his fury. "You lied! You cheated! You made me look a fool! A finish like that and I missed it! How could you be so wrong?"

Karlene watched as he paced the floor, hands clenched, mouth cruel in his anger. A man who had hinted at his love for her now betraying his true motives.

She said, "You know I can never be certain. I've told you that again and again. I scent a node but time is a variable. The one to the west might happen next week or within the next few days." Or never; she had lied as to the scent. Deliberately she let anger tinge her voice. "You demand too much. I gave you the beast-killing. You had scanners set for Albrecht's death."

"Trivialities." With an effort he calmed himself. "Good but not enough—to those who follow the games the end is all-important. I was sure it

66

would happen to the west. I had Thorn set up the scanners. I even told—" He broke off, shaking his head. He had almost said too much. "Five dead," he moaned. "The quarry victorious. And I missed it."

"You had one scanner, surely?"

"One," he admitted. "But the coverage was poor." And would continue to be so without her help. A consideration which smothered his diminishing rage. A mistake, it had to be that, but there would be other opportunities. Smiling, lifting his hands toward her, he said, "Forgive me, my dear. I know you did your best. Blame the artist in me—an opportunity to record a finish like that comes but once in a lifetime."

The artist in him and the greed she could recognize. The tapes he wouldn't be able to sell and the money he had to return to the hunters who, trusting him, had loped to the west. Money in bets and money in blood—God, how had she been so blind?

"You look tense, my dear." His concern was as false as his smile. "You need to relax. A hot bath, perhaps? A massage? Some steam?"

"No," she said. "I'm going downstairs."

The cheers were over, the congratulations, but the party would last until dawn. Dumarest, neat in his normal clothing, his wounds dressed, lifted the glass in his hand as she entered the room in which he held court.

"My lady!" He sipped and added, "It is a pleasure to see you again. How may I know you?"

She smiled at the formal mode of address. "My name? Karlene."

"Just that?"

"Karlene vol Diajiro. Karlene will do." As he handed her a glass of wine she said, "Do I remind you of someone?"

"Why do you ask?"

"You smiled when you first saw me as if—well, it doesn't matter. But I was curious. May I add my congratulations to the rest? If anyone deserved to win the trophy it was you. I assume you are a skilled hunter? None other would have stood a chance. A fighter too, no doubt, it took skill to dispatch those men as you did."

Small talk, flattery, empty words to fill out silence. The ritual used by strangers when meeting other strangers. She felt irritated at herself for emulating the harpies clustered around; painted matrons eager to taste a new delight, others eager to boast of having conquered the conqueror. Why was she acting so awkwardly? A young girl meeting her first man could not have been worse.

Dumarest said, "I had help."

"What?" She blinked then realized he was answering her babble. A man discerning as well as polite. "Help? From whom?"

From those she had never known and would never meet; men who had taught him the basic elements of survival, women who had taught him how to read the unspoken messages carried in gestures and eyes. Others closer to the present; Vellani, the guard, herself.

She shook her head as he mentioned it. "Me? No, you must be mistaken."

"Of course." Dumarest didn't press the point. "Would you care to sit?"

She was tall, her head almost level with his own as he guided her from the room, her flesh cool beneath his hand. Outside a niche held a table and three chairs. Seating her, Dumarest removed the extra chair, setting it well to one side before taking the other. As he settled, a man came bustling toward him, a bottle in his hand.

"Earl! You'll share a drink with me?"

"Not now."

"But—" The man broke off as he saw Dumarest's expression. "I—well, at least accept the wine."

A woman was less discreet.

"Earl, you have my room number. Don't forget it. I'll be expecting you—don't keep me waiting."

As she left, Karlene said, dryly, "To the victor the spoils. I hope you're enjoying them."

"I'm enjoying this." His gesture took in the table, the seclusion, herself. "You were right when you thought you reminded me of someone. You do." He poured wine for them both. "Someone who died a long time ago. I drink to her memory."

"Her name?"

"Derai."

"To Derai!" She sipped and then, following a sudden impulse, drained the glass. "The dead should not be stinted."

"No."

"Nor ever forgotten." Her hand shook a little as she poured herself more wine. "What are we if none remember us when we are gone? Less than the wind. Less than the rain, the sea, the fume of spray. Less than the shift of sand. Nothingness lost on the fabric of time. All ghosts need an anchor."

Friends, a family, children, those who cared. Looking at her, Dumarest saw a lonely woman—haunted by the fear of death.

He said, "You have a way with words. Are you a poet?"

"No, just someone who likes old things. As you do." She smiled at his puzzlement. "The book," she said. "The one you were reading before the game. It looked very old. Did it give you comfort?"

"This?" He took it from his pocket and placed it in her hand. "I found it more a puzzle than anything else. Can you make sense of it?"

She riffled the pages, frowning, shaking her head as she tried to decipher the script.

"It's so faded. Chemicals could restore much of the writing and there are other techniques which could help. Computer analysis," she explained. "Light refraction from the pages—pressure of the stylo would have left traces even though the ink may have vanished. Machines could scan and reconstruct each page to its original content. Later wear could be eliminated." She turned more pages. "This seems to be a personal notebook. I had one when a child. I used to jot down all manner of things: names, places of interest, things I had done. Income and outlay, equations, poetry, all kinds of things. Even secrets." She laughed and reached for her wine. "How petty they seem now."

"The price we pay for growing up. What we thought were gems become flecks of ice. Castles in the sky turn into clouds. The magic in the hills becomes empty space. The secret we thought our own becomes shared by all."

"And childhood dies—as all things must die." She shivered as if with cold and drank some wine. "Why does it have to be like that?"

"Perhaps because we are in hell," said Dumarest. "What better name to give a universe in which everything lives by devouring everything else? Death is the way of life. Only the strong can hope to survive."

"For what? To die?" She sipped again at the wine, feeling suddenly depressed, overwhelmed by the futility of existence. The book moved in her hand and she opened it at random, studying a page with simulated interest. Light, slanting at an angle, enhanced faded script. " 'Earth,' " she said. " 'Up to Heaven's'—something—'door. You gaze'—" Irritably she shook her head. "I can't make it out."

"Try!" Dumarest controlled his impatience. "Please try," he said more gently. "Do what you can."

The wine quivered in the glass he held, small vibrations of nerve and muscle amplified to register in dancing patterns of light. He set it down as the woman frowned at the book.

"It's a poem of some kind. A quatrain, I think. That's a stanza of four lines. You know about poetry?"

"What does it say?"

"The first line is illegible but it must end in a word to rhyme with the last word in the second. My guess is that it goes one-two-four. The third line—"

"What does it say!"

"Give me a minute." She dabbed a scrap of fabric in the wine, wet the page, held it up so as to let the light shine through it. "That's better. Listen." Her voice deepened a little. " 'But if in vain down on the stubborn floor. Of Earth and up to Heaven's unopening door. You gaze today while you are you—how then. Tomorrow when you shall be no more.' No, wait!" She lifted a hand as she corrected herself. That last line reads, 'Tomorrow when you shall be you no more.' "

"Is that all?"

"Yes." She sensed his disappointment. "It would look better set out in lines. It's probably something the owner of the book copied from somewhere. Earth," she mused. "Earth."

He waited for her to say more; to tell him Earth was just a legendary world along with Bonanza and Jackpot, Lucky Strike and El Dorado and Eden and a dozen others. Planets waiting to be found and holding unimaginable treasure. Myths which held a bright but empty allure.

Instead she said, wistfully, "Earth—it has a nice sound. Is there really such a world?"

"Yes." He added, bluntly, "I was born on it. I left it when I was young."

He had been little more than a child, stowing away on a ship, being found, the captain merciful; allowing him to work instead of evicting him as was his right. Together they had delved deeper and deeper into the galaxy when, the captain dead, he had been left to fend for himself on strange worlds beneath alien suns. Regions where the very name of his home world had become a legend, the coordinates nowhere to be found.

"You're lost," said Karlene, understanding. "You want to go home. That is why the book is so important to you. You think it might hold the answer you want."

"The coordinates. Yes."

"Did you really come from Earth?" She leaned toward him, her eyes searching his face. "Would you swear to it? Really swear to it?" As he nodded she added, "This is serious, Earl. It could mean your life."

"I've no need to lie." He caught her wrist, his fingers hard on the pallid flesh. "What do you know?"

"Tomorrow," she said. "I'll tell you tomorrow—after we've deciphered the book."

Cyber Clarge heard the blast of the sirens and lifted his head from the papers he was studying. A curfew? No, it was barely noon and, on Erkalt, sirens did not warn of impending night. A storm? A probability of high order but he was safe within the hotel. A fire, perhaps? Some other catastrophe?

His acolyte brought the answer.

"Master." He bowed as he entered the room. "A matter of local interest. The winds are rising and will establish a pattern yielding unusual phenomena. The sirens are to herald the entertainment."

The window was large, set high in the building, giving a good view of the city and the area beyond. To the south smoke seemed to be rising from the ground, writhing, twisting as it was caught by the winds which buffeted each other and created churning vortexes. Trapped in the blast the snow soared high in a shimmering panorama which filled the air with a dancing chiaroscuro.

Most found it beautiful. Clarge did not.

Against the window he resembled a flame; the scarlet of his robe warm against the snow outside, the great seal of the Cyclan gleaming on his breast. He was tall, thin, his body a functional machine devoid of fat and excess tissue. His face, framed by the thrown-back cowl, held the lineaments of a skull. One in which his eyes burned with a chilling determination.

A man devoid of artistic appreciation; looking at the external spectacle he could see only the waste of natural resources. The winds which blustered so fiercely should be tamed, their energy directed toward the generation of power with which to transform Erkalt into a useful world.

"Master. The information you requested is on the desk."

"Hagen?"

"Has been notified of your wish to see him."

And would report at the earliest opportunity if he was wise. The reputation of the Cyclan was such as to gain them respectful obedience; if he hoped to survive in business or expand his field of operations the entrepreneur would know he had to cooperate to the full. In the meantime other details could be attended to.

A gesture and Clarge was alone, the acolyte, bowing, leaving the room. One unnecessarily ornate with its ornaments and decorations, rugs

and soft furnishings, but Clarge would not order
their removal. Efficiency was not a matter of
trivia but of the skillful application of resources.

Turning from the window the cyber returned
to his desk. The papers he had been studying
were laid out in neat array, those the acolyte had
brought set in a pile to one side. Reports, data,
schedules, statements—details of the past all set
in concrete form. Studying them had given the
cyber one of the only two feelings he could experience; not the glow of mental achievement but
the cortical bitterness of failure.

The bait had been set, the trap sprung—yet
again Dumarest had escaped.

How?

The details were in the reports but they begged
the question. Luck, obviously, and luck of a peculiar kind. The combination of fortuitous circumstances which resulted in a favorable conclusion—
a paraphysical talent which had saved Dumarest
on too many occasions. Small things: the break-
ing of equipment, an illness, a sudden whim on
the part of someone totally unconnected with the
original scheme. Details which, apparently unac-
countably, defeated the main purpose.

This time it had been jealousy.

An emotion Clarge would never experience as
he would never know the impact of love or hate,
fear or anger. Harsh training and an operation
on the thalamus had robbed him of the capacity
of emotion, turning him into a robot of flesh and
blood, dedicated to the pursuit of logic and reason.

The plan should have worked. Instead it had
failed.

The woman, Claire Hashein, selected because of her previous association with Dumarest. The man, Carl Indart, a trained hunter who had to do little but take and hold Dumarest should the need arise. A simple task; legs burned with a laser would have prevented movement. Drugs could have robbed Dumarest of consciousness. Guile could have distracted him until the ship bearing help could have arrived. His ship, his help, the cold decision made by a servant of the Cyclan.

Now he had nothing to report but failure.

Clarge moved a paper, studied another, eyes scanning, brain absorbing the information it contained, assessing it, combining it with other facts, earlier data. Details on which he could base an extrapolation of probable events. The talent of a cyber; the ability to predict the outcome of any situation once in possession of the facts.

"Master?" The acolyte's face showed on the screen of the intercom. "The man Hagen has reported."

"Have him wait."

More papers, further assessment—to operate on speculation and guesswork was unthinkable. Why had the prosecutor allowed Dumarest to volunteer for quarry? The case against him had been incontrovertible and murderers were not normally given such a chance. A need to enhance the games? The advocate's influence? Why hadn't Indart moved to prevent it?

A touch on a button and a screen flared to life on the projector at his side. It was blurred, unsteady, but the figures were plain. Dumarest and

Indart, the latter busy with words. Clarge watched as the scene ended, replayed it, darkened the screen as he sat assessing what the record had yielded.

A man obsessed, who had a monstrous ego— whoever had chosen Indart had been unwise and would pay the penalty for his negligence. As Hagen would pay for knowing more than he should. Had Dumarest guessed the scene was being recorded? Had his question as to the Cyclan been as superficial as it seemed? And the reminder that he was only valuable to the Cyclan if alive—to whom had that been directed?

Certainly Hagen hoped to gain from it.

"I came as fast as I could," he said after the acolyte had admitted him into the cyber's presence. "If there is anything I can do to help just let me know. I want to help—that's why I sent you the recording. Just the part of it I thought would be of interest." Pausing he added, "I know how generous the Cyclan can be."

Clarge said, "Tell me of the woman."

"The one who was murdered? I didn't really know her but—" He broke off, quick with an apology. "I'm sorry. You mean Karlene, don't you? Karlene vol Diajiro. Right?"

"Tell me about her."

"She was a help. Not much of one but she had the looks and the poise and it made it easier to get close to prospects and to make contacts. Window-dressing, mainly. I felt sorry for her. I even offered to take care of her but she didn't take to the idea. Now she's gone."

"Is that all?"

Clarge didn't alter his tone. It remained the same, level modulation devoid of all irritating factors but, as Hagen was about to nod, he felt the impact of the deep-set eyes. A stare which made him feel as if he was transparent and he shifted uneasily in his chair. To lie to the Cyclan was to ask for trouble. To strike a cyber was to commit suicide.

He said, "Not quite. I'll be honest with you. She has a talent. It's pretty wild but I found it useful. She can scent the approach of death." He elaborated the explanation, ending, "That's why she was really useful to me. The rest of it, too, but once we had located a death-node I could really go to town."

"Then why—"

"She cheated!" Hagen's anger spilled over. "The bitch cheated then ran out on me. Just when things were going well and were going to get better. She let me down. Took what she had and left. No warning. Nothing. No chance for me to arrange things. She just ran off with that quarry."

"Dumarest?"

"Who else?"

"You are certain?" Clarge pressed the point. "Absolutely certain?"

Hagen wasn't, he couldn't be, but he lacked the cyber's analytical mind. The pair had vanished and, as far as he knew, had shipped out. That was an assumption, but Clarge estimated it to be correct. He glanced at the reports the acolyte had left; details of ships and their complements, but none carried the names of either the woman or Dumarest. An elementary precaution.

"She sold her furs," said Hagen. "I checked. Took her jewels and all the money she had. Even borrowed on my credit and from my crew. They expect me to pay them. I'll have to see them square even if I have to sell that recording to do it." A hint, one he clumsily emphasized. "It's all I have, you understand. All I've got new."

Clarge said, "Tell me more about the woman. Where did you meet her? When? On which worlds have you operated? Has she any idiosyncrasies? Particular likes or dislikes? Allergies? Habits?" He listened then summoned the acolyte to show his visitor out.

Hagen lingered at the door. "You'll think about my problems? I mean—"

"You will be rewarded."

He, his crew, all who had knowledge of the recording, but it would be a reward they would not appreciate. An accident, an infection, sudden and unexpected death—the Cyclan settled its bills in more ways than one.

Alone Clarge dismissed the matter from his mind as he concentrated on things of greater importance. The woman had accumulated money, probably on Dumarest's advice, and he had cash of his own now augmented by that won with the trophy. Money enough and to spare, money to waste, to burn. Certainly enough to have left false trails.

Had they traveled together or apart?

On which ship?

Heading where?

Questions the cyber pondered as he sat at the desk oblivious to the snow which now hurtled

against the window. The probability that they
were traveling together was high, in the region
of eighty-nine percent; she would not have left
without him and would have seen no point in a
later rendezvous. On which vessel? Three had
left before his own ship had landed; two close
together; the last only recently. Dumarest would
not have waited. The *Tsuchida* or the *Gegishi*?
Hagen had contacted the woman on Ryonsuke
and the *Gegishi* was headed toward that sector of
space.

Would Dumarest abandon the woman once they
had landed?

A probability of high order—but his lead was
small, his destination known and he could not be
certain he was being followed. Even when dying,
Indart had held his tongue.

The woman, Clarge decided. Find the woman
and Dumarest would be close.

There was fire beneath the ice; a burning, hungry demand which left them both exhausted. He
had first known such on Erkalt, then on the
vessel in which they had traveled, now again
here on Oetzer. Rising, Dumarest looked down at
her where she sprawled on the bed. Even in sleep
Karlene was beautiful, the planes of her face
bearing an odd, detached serenity, enhanced by
her pallor, the gleaming mass of her hair.

Silver repeated on her nails, her lashes, the
intricate tattoo above her left breast. A design
almost invisible against the flesh, revealed in
gleams and shimmers when she moved and light
reflected from the metallic ink buried beneath

her skin. The pattern of a flower; slender petals set around a circular center, the whole adorned with curlicues—twelve petals and a circular area quartered by two crossed lines.

A symbol Dumarest had seen before.

"Darling!" She woke as he touched the tattoo. "I've had the most wonderful dream."

"Of home?"

"Of you." Her arms rose to embrace him, pulled him close. "Darling—hold me!"

She sighed contentedly as he obeyed, cradling her head on his shoulder, naked flesh glowing in the diffused sunlight beyond the window of their room. The chamber was large, set with a wide bed and adorned with objects of price. One soft with luxury, scented with delicate odors from cooled and perfumed air that wafted through fretted grills.

The Hotel Brisse was noted for its comfort.

He said, "It's time I was moving. Do you want to sleep longer or—?"

"I'll join you in the shower."

She stood before him beneath the aromatic spray, her fingers touching his torso, following the thin lines of old scars. Brands earned in a hard school where to be slow or weak was to be dead.

"Did it hurt, Earl? When these were made, I mean."

"Did that?" He touched her tattoo.

"I don't know. I can't remember." As before, she dismissed the subject. "But a needle isn't a knife and doesn't cut as deep." Her fingers lingered on his body. "Darling, you must never fight again. Promise me."

"How can I do that?"

Honesty she had learned to admire. Hagen, a score of others she had known would have given the promise without hesitation; lying, treating her like a child. Now, she realized, she was acting like one. Did love always make a woman so stupid?

"I was thinking of the arena." Her hand fell from his chest as she changed the subject. "What are your plans? The book?"

Preoccupied, he didn't answer, prepared himself to go out—alone.

There had been no time to use facilities on Erkalt to decipher the text and further study had yielded little. The man in the laboratory where Dumarest had taken the book the previous day smiled a greeting as he entered.

"My friend! An early bird, I see."

"Did you do as I asked?"

"Of course." The promise of double pay had stimulated his energies. "You could probably get better resolution with more sophisticated equipment but I doubt if it would be worth it. Here." He rested the book on the counter and added a pile of individual sheets. "The pages of the book lacked numbers but I took the liberty of adding them so as to make it easier for you to compare the resolutions with the originals. The marks can be erased quite simply if you wish."

"It isn't important." Dumarest riffled the sheets. The script, enlarged, was far clearer than that in

the book. In places certain words or passages
were tinted red. "This?"

"The computer simulation of what was most
probably present in the original form." The man
swept up the money Dumarest set before him.
"Thank you, sir. Glad to have been of service."

The Hotel Brisse lay to the north. Dumarest
headed south, after leaving the laboratory, following a boulevard flanked with shops, taverns,
casinos, restaurants. He halted at one, taking an
ouside table, a brightly hued umbrella giving
protection from the sun. A waiter served coffee
and cakes, both of which he ignored as he studied
those passing by.

One, a woman, young, her skirt slit to the hip,
mirror dust on eyelids and lips, her blouse care-
lessly open so as to reveal the curves beneath,
slowed, smiling as she saw the book on the table,
the papers set to one side.

"Hi there!" She halted at Dumarest's side. "A
fine day for reading."

"And walking." She didn't take the hint. "You're
wasting your time."

"It's my time. Are you a student?"

"No."

"I didn't think so. You don't look the type.
Lonely, perhaps?" She sighed as he shook his
head. "A shame. Well, no harm in trying." Boldly
she helped herself to a cake. Took another as he
made no objection. "It's a hell of a life when you
can't compete with a book."

He could see the book had a dangerous potential. Had it been set as bait? The tale of Loffredo

a lure to draw him to Erkalt where Claire Hashein and Indart had been waiting? A trap the hunter's rage had aborted—if he had not yielded to jealous fury what would have happened? Dumarest could guess; delay piled on delay giving the Cyclan time to move in. Even had he been sentenced to slave labor no harm would have been done as far as his pursuers were concerned. They could have easily bought his indenture.

Karlene?

Dumarest reached for the papers and found the one he wanted; the one from which she had read. Now the quatrain was clear.

> But if in vain, down on the stubborn floor
> Of Earth, and up to Heaven's unopening Door
> You gaze Today, while You are You—how
> then Tomorrow, when You shall be You no
> more?

Earth—the one word sure to attract his attention. The tattoo she wore—the crossed circle was the astronomical sign of Earth. The hint that she knew of someone who could help him—if he was genuine.

Another trap?

The Cyclan would spare no trouble or expense to recover the secret he possessed, for it would enable them to dominate the known galaxy. It would be logical to pile trap on trap so that, if one failed, another would hold him fast. The Cyclan were masters of logic. They must know of his determination to find the world of his birth.

Was Karlene an agent of the Cyclan?

Dumarest rose and walked farther south to where the landing field sprawled well beyond the edge of town. Oetzer was a busy world and the field was heavy with ships. The air thrummed to the shouts of handlers, yells of porters, the hum of machines loading and unloading vessels eager to return to space. Even as he watched, a siren cut across the babble, and a ship, limned in the blue cocoon of its Erhaft Field, lifted to vanish into the sky.

He could have been on it. He could leave with any ship on the field, and, like them, he would vanish into the sky. Safe from Karlene and any who might be using her.

Safe to do what?

He looked at the field, the ships, seeing not the sleek or battered hulls, but the long, long years of endless travel and frustrated hope. How many more years must he search? How many more worlds must he visit? How many journeys, dangers, gambles must he face and take? And, if Karlene was what she claimed to be, he would have lost the chance now in his hand.

She could lead him to Earth—or she could lead him to death.

Which would it be?

"Earl!"

He turned, freezing the movement of his hand to the knife in his boot. The scarlet she wore was not a robe but a mantle to protect her skin from the growing savagery of the sun. Soon it would be too hot and all work would stop for the siesta.

"Earl!" She halted before him, panting, the mantle casting a warm glow over the pale face shadowed in its hood. "A coincidence but a happy one. I had word and—"

"Word? From whom?"

"The man I told you about." Karlene smiled her pleasure. "It's all right, my darling. He agrees to help you, providing—but you know about that. So I came to find a ship and book passage."

"You?"

"I've engaged a Hausi. He will get us the best and fastest journey." She gestured at the field, the ships standing wide-spaced on the dirt. "It saves time and it's too hot to go shopping around. With luck we could leave tonight." She stared into his face. "What's the matter? Is something wrong?"

"No." He forced a smile. "Nothing."

"Maybe I should have waited," she said. "But I wanted to please you."

Or to sweep him along in the rush of events, giving him no time to think or plan? In turn, he searched her face, seeing the blank stare of mirrored eyes, his own features reflected in the silver lenses she wore.

He said, "Where are we bound?"

"Driest. That's all I can tell you."

A fact he would have learned as soon as he had boarded the vessel and any name she chose to give would be meaningless. Again he searched her face, seeing his own reflection waver a little, blurring as she blinked, vanishing as she turned her head. A time for decision, of knowing that here, now, was the moment of no return.

"Earl? About the booking—did I do right?"

He nodded. A gamble—but all life was that

and he was tired of running, of hiding, of living in dirt and shadows. If Earth was to be found he would find it or die in the attempt.

As the man on Driest would die if he had lied.

Chapter 6

Rauch Ishikari reminded Dumarest of a snake. A tall, slim man, aged, dressed in expensive fabrics which shimmered like scales. His thin, aquiline features bore the stamp of arrogance afforded by position and wealth. His voice, though melodious, bore a trace of cynical mockery. But it was his eyes which dominated the rest: almond slits of enigmatic gray. Set in the creped face they looked like polished shards of stone.

He said, "A final warning, Earl. I have no wish to destroy the innocent."

A chair stood bolted to the floor before the desk behind which he sat. Steel clasps were set in the arms; more on the legs to hold the ankles. The point against which the head would rest was of polished wood. Abruptly it smoked and burst into flame from the invisible beam which ate into the wood. A moment, then the flame was gone, the charred patch a blotch against the rest.

"Lie and the beam will pass through your brain. Are you ready?"

Silently, Dumarest sat in the chair.

He relaxed as the manacles closed to hold him tight. If this was a trap he was in it and there had been no chance to escape. Not from the moment of leaving the vessel when waiting guards had closed in to escort them both to a spired and turreted mansion set high above the town. The palace of a ruler, into which Karlene had vanished leaving him to the ministrations of men more like guards than servants. Then the meeting with Ishikari, the verbal sparring, the abrupt cessation of preliminaries.

Now the manacles, the chair, the laser which, at a touch, would burn out his life.

He said, "You play a hard game, my lord."

"Game? Game? You think this is a game?" Anger edged Ishikari's voice. "If it is you play with your life as the stake!"

"And you?"

Almost he had gone too far and he tensed, watching as the man behind the desk reared, stiffening as if he were a reptile about to strike. There was a long moment during which tiny gleams of light splintered in trembling reflections from the rings he wore, then, as if with an effort, he relaxed.

"I play no game," said Ishikari. "Unless the search for truth be a game. But the path you tread is a dangerous one. Did you tell the woman the truth?"

"About Earth, yes."

"You were born on that world?"

"I was."

"And?"

Ishikari listened as Dumarest went into detail, then fired other questions, probing, inhaling with an audible hiss as Dumarest spoke of the night sky, the moon which looked, when full, like a silver skull. A long time but then it was over, the manacles opening to allow Dumarest to rise. As Dumarest rubbed his wrists his host offered him wine.

"An unusual story," he said, lifting his own glass. "But a true one if the detectors are to be believed. I drink to you, Earl—man of Earth!"

The wine was like blood, thick, rich, slightly warm, traced with a tang of spice and the hint of salt. Dumarest sipped, feeling the liquid cloy on his lips and tongue.

"Earth," mused Ishikari. "A world of mystery. Ask after it and you will be told that it is a legend. A myth. A dream of something which never was. Details bolster that belief; why aren't its coordinates listed in the almanacs? If it is the repository of such enormous wealth why hasn't it yet been found by the expeditions which must have searched for it? Obvious questions but other claims negate them. You know of them?"

The question was like a bullet.

Another test? If so Dumarest passed it. His host nodded as he listened, added his own comments as Dumarest fell silent.

"The mother world from which all men originated—a ridiculous concept when it is remembered how many divergent races inhabit the galaxy. Yellow, white, brown, black—how could one world produce so many different types? We are all one basic race, true, the ability to interbreed proves that, but—"

"We evolved on widely scattered worlds from the impact of space-borne sperm? Seeds driven by the pressure of light to settle on a multitude of planets? Spores which all produced the same basic type?" Dumarest shrugged and sipped at his wine. "I find the one-world concept easier to swallow."

"As a concept, perhaps, but is it the answer?" Ishikari shook his head in doubt. "What to believe? How to unravel the one thread which will guide us through the maze of legend and myth?"

"I thought you had the answer. Karlene said—"

"She told you that I would help you and I will. Follow me."

He led the way into another chamber, one with a high, vaulted roof set with lambent panes now filled with the dying light of day. Tinted squares which threw a dusty shadow over racks of spools, shelved of moldering volumes, oddly fashioned artifacts. Stray beams glinted on metal, crystal, plastic; things which could have been vases or toys or illustrations of tormented mathematical systems. At the far end rested the screen and controls of a computer.

"It is voice-activated," said Ishikari. "I want you to sit at it and tell it all you know about Earth. Everything, each tiny detail, every small item. That and more. All you have learned in your traveling among the worlds." He added, "It

will join other information already in the data
banks. The machine will correlate the information, find associations and meaningful relation-
ships. Determine probabilities and yield valuable
conclusions."

"The coordinates?"

"Perhaps. It's a possibility."

But not good enough. Dumarest looked around
the room, guessing at the guards who must be
watching, the weapons which had him as their
target. A man of Ishikari's position would never
risk his life as he appeared to be doing. Was this
pretense to gain trust? To lull suspicions? Yet
where was the point; if he was in a trap it could
be sprung at any moment.

Casually he moved through the room to a table
which stood against a wall. A convoluted abstract stood at one end. On the other rested
Loffredo's volume and the enhancement he'd had
made.

"You doubt my good faith." Ishikari came to
join him. "I took the liberty of copying your papers, and the computer is assessing the detail
they contained for anything of relative value.
Not proof of my intentions, I admit, but one thing
is. Look." He lifted the sheet bearing the quatrain. "Now this."

He lifted a book from where it rested in the
shadow of the abstract. It was old, thick, stained
with mold and wear. The pages were fretted beneath their protective covering of transparent
plastic. Dimmed illuminations shone with the
ghosts of silver and gold, ruby and emerald. The

script, once thick and black, now sprawled like the gray and tangled web of spiders.

"Look," said Ishikari again, and touched something on the abstract sculpture. Light shone over the book from some source within the convolutions; electronic magic which thickened the script and brightened the hues as if defeating time. "The quatrain. See?" The tip of his finger traced the words. "And here. The word 'Earth' as before." Pages rustled. "Here again, you notice?"

Dumarest said, "What is it?"

"The book? A collection of verse containing pertinent philosophical concepts regarding life and reality." Ishikari riffled the pages. "Life, death and reality. The verse in the book you found shows that. Odd how an itinerant trader could have come by it."

"He could have seen that book." Dumarest gestured to it. "Or one like it."

"A remote possibility. It's more likely he saw it written somewhere. On a wall, perhaps? If so, why?"

Dumarest sensed that he was being led down a path the other had followed before. Spurred to reach a matching conclusion.

"A wall," he said. "But who would write such a verse on a wall unless it was a special place? As a warning? As a concept to bear in mind? A creed, perhaps, or the part of a creed?"

"In which case it surely would have been carved, not written." Ishikari put down the book. "Where would you find such a thing carved on a wall?" He paused, waiting. "A special place," he urged. "You've already mentioned that."

A special place, a carving, a creed. Verses dealing with life, death and reality. Words cut deep into adamantine stone so as to carry their message endlessly through time.

"A church?"

"A temple," corrected Ishikari. "The temple of Cerevox." He add quietly, "I believe it holds the answer we both are seeking."

At dusk Driest became alive with a brash and raucous vitality. Barely had the sun lowered beneath the horizon than lanterns were lit, casting lurid pools of lambent color on pavement and road, the sides of buildings, those thronging the streets and market. Men and women, drinking, laughing, selling produce, skills and, failing all else, themselves.

A crowd in which Dumarest wandered. He had had no trouble in leaving the palace though he was aware of the two men following him at a discreet distance. Guards like ghosts more sensed than seen and he wondered at Ishikari's caution. The bait the man had set was stronger than bars.

"My lords! Ladies! I beg your attention!"

A grating voice accompanied by the clash of metal and Dumarest halted to stare at a peculiar figure. One who wore red, blue, yellow, green—a plethora of vivid hues forming the bizarre depiction of a face. A ragged shape which capered and chanted to the rattle of a sistrum he held in one hand.

"I can dress wounds, treat minor ills, alter a garment. I am adept at massage. I can sing and relate stories to while away the tedium of monotonous hours. I have served as a valet, cook, guard, tutor. I can handle a raft. Hire me and have no regrets."

Next to him stood a vibrant thing which keened; an alien creature from some distant world. It's owner jerked at its leash and, as it reared, snarling, displaying fangs and claws, yelled of its value as a watchdog.

Beyond, a cripple lifted the stump of an arm.

"Lost in the Zhenganian conflict. Supply a prosthesis and I will serve you for a year."

A woman, veiled, silent, the card on her breast telling all she was a bountiful nurse.

Another, young and lissom, who smiled at Dumarest with frank admiration. "My lord? I am trained in the dressing of hair. A seamstress. Hire me for your lady and she will thank you."

He said, "I have no lady."

"Then, perhaps, the greater need of my services. Who else to tend your clothing and give you equanimity of mind?" She stepped a little closer. "Hire me for a month. Test my abilities. A week? A day?" She sighed as he shook his head. "Remember me should you have need."

Dumarest moved on to a plaza where stalls sold refreshments and beggars lay in wait.

"My lord! Give of your charity!"

A man with a face raw with oozing pustles, the orbs of his eyes white with a nacreous film. His bowl remained empty; there were a dozen ways of counterfeiting such sores and the membrane of an egg would emulate true blindness. Another, legless, had better luck. A monk better still.

He stood, his bowl of chipped plastic in his

hand, tall and gaunt in the brown homespun of his robe. His feet were bare but for sandals. His hair, cropped, surmounted a face too old for his years. One with cheeks sunken in deprivation, eyes which stared with compassion at the universe.

"Thank you, brother." He looked at the coins Dumarest had dropped into his begging bowl. "You are generous."

"Your name?"

"Fassar."

"Are you in charge of the Church here?"

"No. Brother Tessio leads us." He added, "Should you wish to ease your heart the church is close to the field."

The usual place but Dumarest had no intention of kneeling beneath the benediction light, of confessing his sins and receiving subjective penance and absolution. Never had he gone through the ritual of a suppliant, not even for the sake of the bread of forgiveness given at its termination. The wafer of concentrate which, to the hungry, was reason enough to feign true remorse.

The monks did not object—each who knelt beneath the benediction light was hypnotically conditioned never to kill. A fair exchange.

Dropping another coin into the bowl he said, "Perhaps you could help me. Cerevox." He repeated the word. "Does it mean anything to you?"

"Cerevox?" The monk thought for a moment, then shook his head. "No."

"Would the others know?"

"I can ask them."

"Please do. Just the monks. I'll ask later at the church."

Dumarest moved on. To one side a stall sold skewers of meat, pasties, spiced bread in flat wedges. It was busy and he passed it then halted at another selling mulled wine. Holding the mug he stood beneath a lantern which bathed him in violet brilliance.

Had Ishikari lied?

If he had he had done it with professional skill. An actor, judging time and emotion, triggering reactive patterns as if he played an organ. Building on Dumarest's natural relief of being freed from the chair and seeing a display of his old things, the talk concerning the computer and then, as if by happy chance, the book and papers and the old volume and the verses it contained.

The temple of Cerevox.

Cerevox?

An odd name but one with a haunting sense of familiarity. Dumarest ran it through his mind; cerevox ... cerevox ... cerevox ... cerevox. Cere. Vox. Cere? Cere?

Erce?

A simple anagram—was that the answer? No, the change made no sense. Ercevox? Vox? Vox?

The monk stood where he had left him. Without preamble Dumarest said, "Vox. The word Vox. What does it mean?"

"I'm not sure. It is very old but, I think, yes, it means voice or voices. I will check if you wish."

"It doesn't matter. And forget the other. Cerevox. Forget it."

Two words, not one, and the simplest of anagrams. Had the meaning intended to be hidden? Or was it a secret known only to those who knew

more than most? Earth had more than one name.
Terra was another. Erce yet another but with a
slightly different connotation. Not just Earth but
Mother Earth. And Vox?

Earth voices? No. The voices of Earth? Not
that either. What then?

Dumarest halted, mind alight with sudden understanding, careless of the crowd around him,
the man who bumped into him and swore then
moved quickly away as he saw his expression.

The Cerevox Temple.

The Voice of Mother Earth!

Karlene's room was on an upper floor, the servant who had guided him running, squealing
away as the panel burst open beneath his boot.

"Earl!" Karlene turned from where she stood
at the side of her bed. Her eyes widened as she saw
his face. "Earl! For God's sake! Don't look at me
like that!"

She backed as he closed the gap between them,
her legs hitting the edge of the bed, her body
toppling, hanging suspended as he caught her
arms and held her against the pull of gravity. In
her eyes he could see the snarling image of his
face.

"I want the truth," he snapped. "All of it. What
is Ishikari to you?"

"A friend. I—" She gasped as he set her jar-
ringly on her feet, mouth opening with terror as
steel shimmered in his hand. "No! Please, no!"

"Talk!" Light shone from the blade as it neared
her throat. An empty threat but she couldn't
know that. "Tell me about Ishikari!"

"He helped me," she said. "A long time ago now. I was in trouble and he helped me."

"And?"

"What do you mean?"

"Did he send you to Erkalt?" He read the answer. "Why?"

"I had—" She broke off, swallowing. "Please, Earl. You're hurting me."

With the threat of the knife, the fingers which left ugly welts on the delicate pallor of her skin. The threat vanished as the blade slid into his boot. The welts would take longer.

He said, less harshly, "He gave you instructions, right? And you can't tell me about them. But you can tell me if you left instructions with the Hausi on Oetzer to use hybeam to radio ahead so that we would be met. Did you?" Her nod was an admission. "Did you tell him to radio anyone else? The Cyclan?"

"No. No, Earl, I swear it!"

"What do you know of the temple?" He saw the sudden laxness of her face. "Damn it, girl! I won't hurt you. Just tell me about Cerevox."

From behind him Rauch Ishikari said, "You're wasting your time, Earl. She can't."

He stood within the room, guards flanking him at the rear, the snouts of their weapons ready to lower a barrier of destruction from either side.

Dumarest said, "If they fire they will kill the woman. You wouldn't want that."

"Would you?"

"No."

"Then we are agreed." Ishikari stepped to one side his hand gesturing toward the door. "I can find us a better place in which to talk. If you will precede me?"

A matter in which he had no choice; beneath the empty courtesy lay the cold determination of steel. The passage was empty, a door standing open a short way down. The room held a table, chairs, ornaments, a flagon of wine and glasses on a tray. Wine which could have been drugged. Dumarest shook his head as Ishikari gestured for him to help himself.

"I'd rather talk."

"About Karlene? What do you want to know." Before Dumarest could begin Ishikari lifted a hand. "First let me explain something. There are certain things she cannot talk about. I mean that literally. As a child she was conditioned never to reveal certain things about herself. You have seen her tattoo? Asked her about it? She couldn't answer you. Couldn't remember. Am I correct?"

"Perhaps. She dodged the question."

"As she did when you asked her about the temple?" Ishikari stepped to the flagon and helped himself to wine. Lowering his glass he said, "She *cannot* answer that question. Demand a reply and she will escape into fugue."

A loss of memory in which she left reality. A safeguard against her betraying secrets—but there were ways to break such conditioning. Had Ishikari found such a method?

Dumarest looked at the man. The wine he sipped was a demonstration of its harmlessness or an act to lull Dumarest's suspicions. As his own demonstration of violence had been designed to gain quick answers. If nothing else it had brought his host running, eager to guard the woman or the knowledge she held.

He said, bluntly, "Can you?"

"Answer the question? No, but I can guess. When young, perhaps only a child, she was bound to the temple. Later she was forced to leave or she may have escaped. When my agent found her she was working with a fortune teller who claimed the ability to predict the moment of death. You are aware of her talent?" As Dumarest nodded, Ishikari continued, "It is wild but was good enough to impress the clients of the charlatan. My agent bought her and sent her to me. Once she was established I tried to question her but—" His shrug was expressive.

Dumarest said, "Then you have no real proof she was ever connected with the temple."

"There is the tattoo. Twelve petals surrounding a circle quartered by a cross. You know what that signifies. Look closer and you will see that the cross is set within a pentagram. Five sides, one for each of the senses, the common hallmark of humanity. The curlicues resemble schematics. The twelve petals symbolize—"

"The Sign of the Zodiac," snapped Dumarest. "That still isn't proof. Anyone can copy a tattoo."

"I have other evidence. The association is undeniable. She was attached to the temple and must know what it contains."

The answer to where Earth was to be found but, Dumarest sensed, Ishikari hoped for more. He stood by the table, apparently calm, but the wine in the glass he held quivered a different message. Then, as if aware of the betrayal, he set down the container.

Dumarest said, "Was Karlene indentured? You said your agent bought her."

"The charlatan claimed debts due to maintenance. It was easier to pay than argue. She was found on Threndor—a world of the Sharret Cluster."

"I want to see her."

"No. She must not be bullied."

"I want to apologize, not threaten. I was a little rough with her." A mistake, the shock hadn't achieved its objective. Dumarest added, "I might even be able to find out what you want to know."

"I told you—"

"Fugue, yes, but there are more ways than one of reaching the truth. I could be lucky—and what have you to lose?"

She sat in her room like a broken doll, a toy used and discarded, slumped on the edge of her bed, head lowered, face hidden by the cascade of her hair. Dumarest touched it, caressed the fine strands, the soft flesh of her naked arms. Beneath his fingers he felt the jerk and twitch of muscles. A woman locked in the grip of conflicting emotions. A child, lost, bewildered, needing help.

To the maid standing by he said, "Leave us."

"But—"

"Do it!"

As she obeyed Dumarest sat at Karlene's side, his thigh touching her own, one arm around her shoulders, the other parting the hair before her face. Tears marred her cheeks and her lips held the moist looseness of a frightened child.

"Karlene." His tone was gentle, soothing. "Come back to me, darling. Come back now. Wake up and join me. I need you. Come back to me. Karlene, come back to me."

"Earl?" Her voice was small, empty. "Earl?"

"You're safe, darling. Nothing can hurt you. There's no need to hide." He continued speaking, words which formed a comforting drone as his hands stroked her hair, her body. The treatment he would give to a frightened animal. "Come back to me, Karlene. Come back to me."

"Earl?" Her voice was stronger as she turned toward him. Emptiness vanishing as if she woke from sleep. "Is that you, darling?" Her hands groped, found his, closed with crushing intensity. "You attacked me. I thought you were going to kill me. A dream. Was it a dream?"

"I asked you a question. Don't you remember?"

"No."

"It seemed to upset you."

"Why should it do that?"

"I don't know. Tell me about your life on Threndor. The man you worked for before you joined Ishikari. How did you meet?"

"He found me. He must have found me. I was lost and cold and frightened and . . . and. . . ." She shook her head, frowning. "I can't remember."

"Never mind. Did he ever talk about your past? Ask what you'd done before you met?"

"I don't think so. No."

"Wasn't he curious?" Dumarest waited then said, gently, "Surely he must have wanted to know something about you. A beautiful young girl. Others could have been looking for you. There could have been the possibility of a reward." Casually he added, "How old were you when you met?"

"I don't know. I don't think he liked me much. Not before he found out about—" She fell silent then, in a different tone, said, "I don't want to talk about it."

"Then we won't."

"Not now. Not ever."

"I understand." Dumarest freed his hand from the woman's grasp. "I wish you could trust me as much as you trust Ishikari."

"What do you mean?"

"Surely he must have asked you about your past? He took you in, looked after you. Maybe you're related in some way. Why did he send you to Erkalt?"

"I was working. With Hagen. You know that."

"But you told Ishikari about me. Why?"

"You needed help. He said he could help you. You agreed to meet him. You know all this."

Dumarest said, "What I don't know is what he wants. What he hopes to find. Why is he so interested in the temple?" He saw the sudden blankness of her eyes. "Karlene! Stay with me!"

"I'm sorry." She drew a shuddering breath. "I feel confused. All these questions. "Earl—what do you want of me?"

"Answers. About Ishikari. Don't you remember the questions he asked? The details he wanted?"

Her face gave the answer. She remembered

Ishikari's probing no more than she remembered his own recent violence. The fugue into which she escaped blurred the cause of its creation and turned real events into the figment of a dream.

Chapter 7

By day the church was bright with pennons of blue and white; colors of purity and hope. At night lanterns of the same hues signaled to all that here was to be found help and comfort both of body and mind. And, always, throngs came to partake of both.

Brother Tessio walked among them, tall, austere in his brown robe and sandals. A costume designed for utility, devoid of ostentation. Not even the heads of the great establishments wore a different garb. Not even those who ruled the great seminaries on Peace and Hope. The Church of Universal Brotherhood had no use for hypocrisy; a jewel would buy food for the starving, gold braid provide medicine for the sick, expensive fabrics make a mockery of the humility which alone could alleviate the suffering of humanity.

"Brother!" A woman caught at his hand. "Please

help me. My child—" The small bundle beside her stirred with a fitful wailing. "Please!"

"You will be seen," promised Tessio. "And the child will be helped."

With medicines, antibiotics, drugs. With the skill of monks trained in manipulation, hypnosis, natural healing. As the others waiting in the annex would be helped and sent on their way. Some would leave a donation; others, too poor to give even that, would mouth thanks; and some would offer their labor at menial tasks.

But none would ever be refused.

Tessio sighed as he reached the far end of the room and passed through a door into a passage. From behind drawn curtains he heard the murmur of voices and lingered at the cubicle containing Brother Vendell. A good man, if inclined to be impatient. One who chafed at the irksome necessity of making haste slowly.

"Look into the light," he heard the monk say to the suppliant kneeling before him. "Relax. Concentrate on the colors. See how they shift and change. The patterns they make. Try to follow them. So soft. So restful. Watching them makes you feel so relaxed, so tired ... so tired ... tired. ..."

There was the hint of the mechanical in the voice and Tessio made a mental note to speak to Vendell about it. To deal with the endless line of suppliants could not help but be boring but never, ever, should it be shown as that. Each was an individual and needed to be reassured of his or her particular importance.

Pride, concern, consideration—words Tessio

turned in his mind as he went on his way. Pride in personal ethics, concern for the general environment, consideration for all other individuals. If men would keep their word, cease from wanton destruction, have the imagination to realize how their actions affected others. If each could look at others less fortunate and say "There, but for the grace of God, go I," the millennium would have arrived.

Something he would never see. No monk now living would ever see—men spread too fast and wide for that. Yet it was the objective for which he strived and to which the Church was dedicated.

"Brother!" The monk was young, still idealistic, yet to experience the full measure of pain and degradation which was the inevitable price paid by all who aspired to wear the brown robe. "You have visitors."

They waited in a small room containing a table, chairs, a patchwork rug on the floor. The walls were bare aside from a crude painting, a mask carved from wood, a bundle of thin reeds, a knife made from flints set into a scrap of wood. Mementoes, each with its history and each punctuating a period of his life. Tessio would use them if the need arose; making conversation, illustrating various points as he strove to reach the heart of a problem. No monk of his standing was less than a master in applied psychology.

Dumarest saved him the trouble. Rising to his feet as the monk entered, he said, "Brother, we need your help."

"We?" Tessio glanced at Karlene where she sat. "You speak for both?"

"Yes." She met his eyes, her own direct. "I am under no duress but—" She broke off, hands together, knuckles taut beneath the pallor of her skin. "Earl, do you think this wise? I mean—"

He said, abruptly, "Tell me about Cerevox."

Tessio inhaled as she slumped, face lax, eyes rolling upward beneath her lowering lids. Dumarest caught her, steadied her in the chair. His touch, Tessio noted, was gentle, almost a caress.

"An illustration," said Dumarest. He straightened, one hand holding the woman upright in her chair. "Do you know what you're looking at?"

"Fugue." Tessio touched the pale skin of her throat and forehead, lifted an eyelid, pressed a finger beneath the cascade of her hair. "A natural infirmity?"

"Artificial."

"Conditioning?"

"Yes. She has been deliberately sensitized against certain words or concepts and acts, as you have seen, when stimulus is applied. I want you to remove that sensitivity." Dumarest saw the doubt in the monk's eyes. "Listen," he said urgently, "She is under no duress—she told you that. She is here of her own volition. She is sick and asks for your help. If what you believe has any validity at all—how can you deny her?"

A good question but the answer was not so simple. The man was what he appeared to be but the woman wore fabrics of price and could be under emotional constraint. Too old to need the consent of a guardian but should he arouse the anger of her family the Church would suffer. If it was abolished from this world who would help those now waiting for succor?

One against many and yet . . . and yet. . . .

There, but for the grace of God, go I!

Dumarest said, quietly, "If I brought you a bird with a broken wing what would you do? Kill it? Heal it? Ignore it and leave it to suffer? Tell me."

"This woman is not a bird."

"She is still a cripple. An emotional one, true, but a cripple just the same. I'm not asking you to find out who applied the conditioning, or when, or why. I'm asking you to remove it. To heal her as you would heal an injured bird. To make her whole again. To give her free choice. To restore her pride."

Pride which, if it became overweening, would be a sin. As concern for another would become if allowed to grow into interference. As consideration could never be.

Could he show less consideration to a woman than he would to a bird?

Tessio said, "I can promise nothing. I will do my best but my skill is limited. You must understand that."

"You will help?"

"I will do what I can."

Dumarest waited in the annex, striding down the rows of those wanting aid, disturbing them and the attendant monks both. A thing he recognized and he left the church to stand looking at the field. The perimeter lights made a harsh circle of brilliance around the area, small glitters reflected from the barbed points of the mesh. A hard fence to climb; too high to jump and the barbs would rip flesh and clothing. Guards stood at the gate and others, not so obvious, stood close in the shadows. Men without uniforms but with watchful eyes and Dumarest had no doubt as to their orders. They, the lights, the savage barbs were all a part of his cage.

As was Karlene herself.

He moved on, edging around the church as he thought of her. Imagining her face beneath the glowing, ever-changing colors of the benediction light. Tessio would be using his skill and trained ability, questioning, suggesting, directing. Easing the burden others had clamped on her mind. The guardians of the temple? The charlatan she had worked for? Others?

A wall rose before him and he turned to retrace his steps. It would have been easier for the guardians to have killed. Safer, too, if their secrets were so important, her knowledge so dangerous. The charlatan would have had no reason. A pretense? The fugue had been genuine enough. The conditioning was real. But who had established it? And why?

"Brother?" A young monk headed toward him. "If you would return to the church?"

Karlene waited in the room in which he had left her. She turned as he entered, radiant, smiling, arms lifting to merge into his embrace.

"Darling! I feel so well! So alive!"

"I'm glad." Dumarest touched the softness of her cheek, her hair, his fingers imparting kisses. They were alone. Tessio, as well as being a psychologist, was also a diplomat. "Tell me about Cerevox. The Temple of Cerevox."

"What?" She stared at him, frowning, and for a moment he wondered if the monk had failed. But there was no sign of withdrawal. No hint of fugue. Then she smiled. "Cerevox? Of course, darling. What do you want to know?"

It was the fabrication of a dream; a mass of chambers and passages, of halls and promenades, open spaces and soaring pinnacles. An edifice of stone which had grown during the course of time to rest like a delicate flower in the cup of misted hills.

Dumarest pictured it as he sat in the tavern to which he had taken Karlene. A mental image enhanced by the dancer who spun with a lithe and supple grace to the music of pipe and drum. The fabrics she wore echoed the vibrant hues of gems set to adorn arch and pillar, the tinkle of her bells the clear chimes of instruments stirred by the wind. The pipe and drum matched the tramp of marching feet, the chant of devoted worshipers. Even the serving maids emulated young and nubile priestesses.

"It is beautiful," said Karlene. "I can't begin to tell you how beautiful it is. The wind is always gentle. The air is always warm. At night the sky is a blaze of stars. There are two moons and, when they are close, there are ceremonies."

"Special ones?"

"Yes. To the Mother.

"How about those who live there?"

"All are bound to the Temple. Some gather

fruits and tend the land. Some build. Others weave
fabrics for robes and garments. The elders teach.
Those who come to make their devotions bring
offerings. Usually it is money or goods of value.
Sometimes they offer the fruit of their bodies."

"Children?"

"Those barely able to walk. They are examined
by the priests and, if found to be without flaw, are
bound to the Temple." Her hand rose to touch the
place above her left breast. "If accepted they bring
honor."

Dumarest said, "Who are these devotees? The
Original People?"

"Who are they?"

"A religious sect with a mania for secrecy. They
neither seek nor welcome converts; new adher-
ents are gained from natural increase." Watching her, he quoted, in a tone which held the roll
of drums, "From terror they fled to find new
places on which to expiate their sins. Only when
cleansed will the race of Man be again united."

Karlene said, frowning, "What does it mean?"

"It's part of the creed of the Original People.
Do you recognize it? No? A pity. Once things
happen as they say there should be a paradise
like the one you've described. The Temple," he
explained. "I can't understand why anyone should
want to leave it."

"Are you saying I lie?"

"I'm saying I'm curious. You agreed to talk.
What happened? Why did you leave?"

"I didn't fit. I wasn't wanted." Her tone was
tense, hurt. "And I grew worried. I kept feeling

that thing in my mind. At first I asked about it then I just kept it to myself."

"Why?"

"They told me I was imagining things. That I was contaminated. I knew what happened to contaminated things and I was frightened it would happen to me. I thought it was going to happen, that I was going to die in the fire like the other things. The dead animals and spoiled fruits so ... so...." She broke off and took a deep breath. Then, in a calmer, more adult tone said, "So I left. I disguised myself and mingled with a bunch of worshipers. I was lucky—when a man discovered I didn't belong I made him believe I was on a secret mission for the Temple. He aided me."

As had others in ways and for reasons Dumarest didn't go into. The charlatan had provided a temporary refuge. Rauch Ishikari a more permanent one. But what was his real interest in the Temple?

"He wanted me to describe it," said Karlene when he asked. "In detail. He wanted to know all about me, everything I'd done. He made me tell him about the rituals and—"

"Made you?"

"He kept on and on. It was easier to talk than remain silent. Anyway, I owed him. He was good to me. I wanted to help as much as I could. Then, I guess, he must have lost interest or grown tired of asking questions because he let me live much as I wished."

The dancer finished her performance to a burst of applause and left the floor, bowing, an assistant gathering up the coins thrown in appreciation of her skill. A tumbler replaced her, a man who spun and twisted in a glitter of sequins. One who kept shining balls balanced in the air above head and feet.

As Ishikari had kept the truth spinning just beyond his reach.

It had to be Ishikari.

Dumarest looked at his hands, at the goblet he held between them. Wine he didn't want but its price had paid for the shelter of the tavern, the privacy he had needed. Time to learn what he could away from prying ears and eyes but it had been little enough, as his host must have known. Was he even now smiling at his jest?

If so it was time to wipe the grin off his face.

He sat in the chamber with the vaulted roof, the panes now dark with the nighted sky. Lanterns glowed from brackets set high on the walls, their light adding to the nacreous glow from the computer. Limned against the screen Ishikari looked thin and insubstantial, then he moved, light splintering in dying reflections from gems and precious metal, the braid edging the fabric he wore so that, for a moment, he was adorned with glinting scales.

"My friend." His gesture dismissed the guard attending Dumarest. "You are impetuous."

"Impatient." Dumarest strode closer to the screen, his host. "Why did you lie?"

"Did I?"

"The conditioning—"

"Was applied by me, true, but did I ever tell you otherwise?"

"You told me she had been conditioned when a child."

"As she was. Surely you must have realized that. How did she describe the Temple? As a paradise, right? Warm air and gentle winds and all the rest of it. What else was that but a picture impressed on her mind when young? Tell a child often enough that dirt is bread and he will believe it. Heat will become cold, stench become perfume, pain turn into pleasure. As for the rest?" Ishikari shrugged. "A man is a fool who doesn't guard his treasure."

"You sucked her dry," said Dumarest. "Learned all you could then made sure she wouldn't be able to talk to others. Why didn't you stop me? You must have known I'd taken her to the monks."

"Of course. I would have been disappointed if you had not."

"You wanted me to question her?"

"I want you to believe," said Ishikari. "In her. In me. In what I have to tell you. Cerevox is real but, like Earth, not easy to find. Did you ask her where it was?"

"She didn't know. She thought the world and the Temple had the same name."

"They haven't. Cerevox is located on Raniang. It is a world of the Sharret Cluster."

"As Threndor is," said Dumarest. "She didn't travel far."

"Farther than you think." Ishikari touched a button on the computer. As the screen flared he said, "The Sharret Cluster."

The answer came in a mellifluous female voice

which matched the graphic symbols illuminating the screen.

"The Sharret Cluster: central coordinates 42637/69436/83657. A collection of thirty-eight suns in close proximity together with strands of cosmic dust. There are a multitude of worlds most of which have neither been explored nor noted. A total of twenty-seven are habited some with only minor installations. In alphabetical order they are—"

"Cease! Name only major worlds."

"In order of population-destiny based on the latest almanac-entries: Dorgonne, Brauss, Stimac, Berger, Threndor—"

"Cease! Where does Raniang lie? In population order?"

"Nineteenth."

"Position in relation to Threndor? In spatial terms."

"Almost diametrically opposite in cluster."

"A long way," commented Ishikari as the computer-screen resumed its blank glow. "And none of it easy. Can you imagine what it was like to a young girl, frightened, totally unsuited to what she went into? It must have been a living nightmare."

One Dumarest had known. He said, "What is your interest in the Temple?"

"The same as yours."

"I doubt it. I want to find Earth. I think you want to find something else. Why else all your questions as to robes and rituals? Just what does Cerevox mean to you?"

For a long moment Ishikari made no answer,

then, abruptly, he said, "You know of the Original People?"

"Yes."

"Their creed?" As Dumarest nodded, he continued, "From terror they fled. Terror. Or maybe it should be Terra. Another name for Earth as you must know. A slight change, natural enough, but one word becomes another. Now, if we say, From Terra they fled—you grasp the significance?"

"They left Earth, yes."

"But why?" Ishikari leaned forward as if he were a snake about to strike. "They fled—from what? They ran and settled on other places. Those other places could only have been worlds. And the cleansing they mention. The need to expiate their sins. What sins? Against whom?" Pausing he added, "And why should Earth have been proscribed?"

"You know?"

"Don't you?" Ishikari rested his hand on the computer. To it he said, "On the basis of all information you have, give the most probable location of the mythical planet Earth."

The screen flared, became a mesh of drifting lines, of slowly rotating graphics and transient figures. A background to the mellifluous voice.

"The firmest guide to the location is the zodiac. The zodiac consists of twelve symbols, each representing a portion of a band of the sky in a complete circle. A configuration of stars represents each of the symbols. Earth is supposed to lie within the center of the circle. The signs are: Ram, Bull, Twins, Crab, Lion, Virgin, Scales, Scorpion, Archer, Goat, Pot, Fish. The point in space from which these signs are recognized in a surrounding circle is the most probable location of Earth."

"The actual design of the configurations?"

"Unknown."

"Give details of all other worlds which have been proscribed."

"None."

Dumarest said, "How do you know Earth was proscribed?"

"The fact worries you?" Ishikari touched the computer and, as his hand fell from the control, added, "I found a reference in an old book. There is also a mention in the Cerevox rituals, but you wouldn't know about that. Now, given the findings of the computer, could you find Earth?" He smiled as Dumarest shook his head. "Of course not. The clue of the zodiac is useless. The patterns to look for are unknown and even if we had the information where would we start? The books tell us nothing. Those to which we have access, at least. To me it is obvious that all references to Earth were deliberately suppressed and all almanacs giving its location destroyed. How else to proscribe a world other than by isolating it? And again we come to the question—why? Why was a world abandoned? Condemned?"

The answer he hoped to find. His real interest in the Temple. Dumarest wondered why he had made no reference to his failure to add his own information to the computer, then decided Ishikari had either forgotten his command or thought it had been obeyed. The latter, he decided, the man was not accustomed to disobedience.

"The Original People," said Ishikari. "They have the answer, I'm sure of it. They have kept the past alive. Distorted, altered, wrapped around with symbolism and myth, but the truth is in their keeping. All we have to do is find it."

"How? They value their secrecy."

"But you know of them and so do I?"

"Fanatics existing on backward worlds," said Dumarest. "Small groups living in primitive conditions. Everyone knows that."

"How?" demanded Ishikari. "If they are so secret how do we know even that? No, my friend, nothing is so secret that it cannot be learned by others. The Original People know that. Know too that a secret that is not a secret is safe. I confuse you? Tell me, how better to keep a secret than by persuading everyone that it isn't really a secret at all? Look for your primitives and you fail to see the civilized men beneath your nose. The primitives are hard to find, true, but who wants to find them anyway? Who really has interest in a bunch of fanatics conducting bizarre and esoteric rituals? And yet, in order to maintain cohesion, certain ceremonies must be maintained."

"The Temple?" said Dumarest. "Cerevox?"

"The heart of the Original People. The center of their worship. I am certain of it." Ishikari left the computer and moved with long, loping strides. A man burning with conviction. He halted and caught at the edge of a table while sucking air deep into his lungs. More quietly he said, "I have been advised against exciting myself but at times I forget."

"You are ill? Shall I call for help?"

"No."

"Is there anything I can do?"

"Listen. For now just listen." Ishikari drew more air into his lungs. "Mysteries have always fascinated me. Even as a boy I yearned for answers. My position makes it impossible for me to follow a scientific pursuit but, even so, it has compensations. I can question and those I question know better than to lie. I can order and be obeyed. I can punish and I can reward. Do I make myself clear?"

Power displayed as the threat of a naked blade and his own position made obvious. Dumarest waited, saying nothing.

"Cerevox is a mystery and one I intend to solve. I want to know what lies at the heart of the Temple." Ishikari paused to breathe, his hand tight on the edge of the table. "Think of it! The secret they have guarded for so long. Not just the location of Earth but all the rest. Why was it abandoned? Why proscribed? What terrible sin needs to be expiated? The answers can be found. You will find them."

He stared at Dumarest, his eyes wide, bright, glowing with fanatical determination. Foam showed at the corners of his mouth.

"You will find what lies at the heart of the Temple," he said. "And, finding it, you will discover how to find Earth."

Chapter 8

Ellen Contera was as dark as Karlene was fair. A small, hard, self-assured woman with close-cropped hair, a face which showed her age and a restless, impatient manner.

To Dumarest she said, "So you're the appointed. How good are you with that knife?"

He smiled, not answering, looking at the enclosed garden they were in: a walled extension of the palace, the walls high and topped with vicious spikes. A stone promenade followed the inside of the wall, shrubs and bushes edging it to surround an inner lawn set with a band of flowering plants. The air was soft, scented, the heat trapped from the noon sun reflected from the walls and created shimmers in the air.

"I asked you a question." Ellen moved three paces, halted, moved back to the bench against which she had been standing. The fabric of her clothing made a dry rustling. She wore pants, shoes, a mannish blouse. Her hands, broad, the fingers spatulate, were marred with livid blotches. She wore no rings. "Need I repeat it?"

"You made a statement and asked a question," corrected Dumarest. "One I don't have to answer. Why did you say I'm the appointed?"

"Rauch gave us the word. You're going to lead the team to rob the Temple. Didn't he tell you?" She frowned as he shook his head. "Did you think you'd be operating alone?"

A possibility he had considered during the night—but had rejected. To a madman all things were simple and Ishikari, he guessed, was far from sane. He remembered the eyes, the glare, the foam on the lips. A man obsessed. A dreamer driven insane by his dream. Such a man was dangerous in more ways than one. Rather than follow him Dumarest had decided to go his own way.

"He's consumed with an ideal," said the woman. "But I guess you noticed that. For years he's been trying to solve the mystery of Cerevox. I've helped him. The girl," she explained. "Karlene vol Diajiro. A mess if ever I saw one. God knows what they did to her in the Temple but I managed to bury most of the traumas."

"You?"

"I'm Ellen Contera. Profesor of applied psychology. Doctor of medicine. Doctor of hypnotic therapy. Professor of psyche manipulation. I'm among the top of my field. Something else you didn't know, eh?"

"No." There had been pride in her voice when

she had mentioned her name and titles. "Why does Ishikari need me?"

"If I'm so good?"

"I didn't say that."

"No, you didn't." Her eyes searched his face. "The answer's simple: I work in one way and you in another. That's why I asked if you could handle that knife." She paused as if expecting him to demonstrate, then, as he made no attempt either to speak or reach for the blade, continued, "He's been looking for the right kind of man. One with guts, courage and intelligence. He figures you fit the bill."

Dumarest said, dryly, "I gained the impression he wanted a thief."

"He has a thief. Someone caught trying to rob the palace. He's alive now only because he was so good. You'll meet him later. For now I'd like to know how you feel about it."

"Robbing the Temple?"

"Call it that if you like. I was thinking about the religious aspect. Some men can't kill. Some can't stand the sight of another in pain. Some won't commit sacrilege. We all have our weaknesses. Are you superstitious?"

"No."

"Does the thought of violating a sacred shrine bother you?" As Dumarest shook his head she said, "I'd like to check your psyche. Would you object to hypnotic interrogation? It would do no harm."

"To you, no."

"Then you object?"

"Strongly. I don't like anyone probing my mind. Call it a weakness if you like."

"I'd call it a strength." Again she strode from the bench, but this time did not return. "Well? Aren't you interested in what's facing you?"

She led the way from the garden into a room bright with diffused sunlight. Cold air gusting from vents gave the place a stimulating coolness. In the center of the chamber stood a large table. On it was the model of a patch of countryside together with a building.

"That's it," said Ellen. "The Temple of Cerevox."

It wasn't what Dumarest had expected.

Karlene had described a place of delicate construction, of walks and promenades, soaring arches and open spaces filled with the perfume of massed flowers. The spaces were present together with the walls but the spaces were bare and the walls had been constructed of rough stone which sprawled in a mazelike pattern around the central mass of the building, which was low, domed, set with stunted towers and flanked by the sloping roofs of attendant buildings.

"No gems," said Ellen. "No polished stone. No soaring arches, flowers, scented air. And you can forget about the warm air and gentle winds. Raniang isn't known for clement weather."

"She lied."

"Karlene? No. She told you what she thought to be the truth."

"Conditioning?"

"From the moment she was bound to the Temple. The rituals are strongly hypnotic. They usually are, of course, but these are something special.

Chants, drums, incense, suggestion, fasting, pain, soporifics—they use the whole spectrum and they're damned good at what they do. First they blurred her early memories then imposed a false reality. She told you they only accept the very young?"

"Those barely able to walk."

"That, in itself, is suspicious." Ellen gestured at the table, the model it carried. "What would they want with people so young? Children are a burden until they can at least fetch and carry. The Temple needs servants, workers, guards and a supply of new priests and priestesses. Those in charge would have neither the time nor resources needed to bring up the very young and helpless."

"So you dug into her mind," said Dumarest. "You and Ishikari. And found, what?"

"I did the digging, she only thinks Rauch did. And what I found isn't nice. She must have been about eight or nine when they took her. Suggestion made her think the air was warm and all the rest of it. An invented paradise to keep her and the rest happy. Fair enough—on a world like Raniang that's good therapy. But later, when her talent began to worry her, things changed for the worse. Can you tell me how and why?"

She was serious. Looking at her Dumarest recognized the expression in her eyes, the blank attentiveness of her face. Another test? One to determine his level of intelligence?

He said, "She was in a closed society. A religious one. For such a society to work all must share the same beliefs and have an unquestioning obedience to authority. Her talent would have set her apart."

"And?"

"Differences, in such a society, cannot be tolerated. All must conform."

"You've got it!" Ellen turned, relaxing, and he guessed he had passed her test. "To them she became a heretic. Her talent was a nagging ache; a question to which she could find no answer. Instead of trying to understand it they tried to eradicate it. To beat it out of her." Her voice thickened a little. "I mean that literally. I'll spare you the details but there are none so cruel as the righteous. If Karlene hadn't run they would have killed her."

"So the story she told me—"

"Was the edited version of what I put in her mind." Ellen gestured at the table. "What do you think? Can you get in there and find what it contains?"

Dumarest said, "I'll need a lot more information before I can answer that."

"You'll get it. Now come and meet those who are going with you."

The thief was Ahmed Altini, a slim, lithe man with a solemn face and grave eyes. His hands were designed to handle locks as a surgeon handled a scalpel. Neat hands, deft, the kind Dumarest had seen often before. Gambler's hands trained to manipulate cards.

One touched his own in greeting. "An old custom," Ahmed explained. "But one we must become accustomed to using."

"The pilgrims use it." Kroy Lauter was big, bluff, one cheek pocked with scars. "But I'll greet you in a more familiar fashion." He extended both hands, palms upwards in a mercenary's welcoming salute.

Ramón Sanchez smiled as he stepped forward. A fighter, light on the balls of his feet, shoulders hunched as if ready to drop into a familiar crouch. His touch was cool, assured.

"We are of a kind, it seems. Unlike Dietz."

Pinal Dietz was an assassin, a stealer of lives as Altini was a stealer of wealth. A small, neat, precise man devoid of any outstanding feature. One who would be easily lost in a crowd and as quickly forgotten by any who saw him. Only at times, when his eyes betrayed him, did he look what he was.

"A gambler," he said. "Although he's tired of the risks a gambler must take. Once we have won the wealth of the Temple I shall retire to some secluded world. I may even write a book."

"On the art of killing?" Ellen gave him no time to answer. "Rauch had him hired," she explained to Dumarest after she had drawn him to one side. "Paid to kill a man from whom he wanted a favor. He warned the man what to expect and, when Pinal made his attempt, he was taken. The victim, of course, was grateful. Pinal decided to work for Rauch rather than face the penalty of failure."

"Ishikari trusts him?"

"Now, yes." Her smile was enigmatic. "An elementary precaution. Pinal is a snake without fangs until given the word. I shall teach you that word."

"The others?"

"Ahmed you know about. Kroy is what he seems—a mercenary willing to do anything for the hope of reward. Ramon comes from the arena which is why I asked if you were good with a knife. Such a man may decide to question your authority." She glanced to where he stood with the others. "Come, now, let's eat."

The room was next to the one holding the model; a spacious chamber containing tables, chairs, a bookshelf and computer terminal. A door opened to baths and showers. One table bore scattered cards; another, chessmen in neat array. The center table, flanked by chairs, bore wine and plates of succulent dainties. Salvers bore cold meats and an assortment of bread and pastry.

As he helped himself Kroy said, "What do you think we'll find in the Temple, Earl?"

"Probably nothing."

"What?"

"He could be right." Altini helped himself to wine. "I once robbed a shrine on Matsuki. It was reputed to hold a fabulous treasure. A thing so holy that it was virtually beyond price. I found an egg."

Kroy stared his disbelief. "An egg?"

"Just that. It was made of stone."

"A jewel? Well—"

"Stone," repeated the thief. "Some hard, black stone. Smoothed and polished, of course, but about as valuable as any other you can pick up on the shore. A symbol valuable only to those who worshipped it." He sipped his wine with the fastidiousness of a cat. "I could tell you other stories."

"We can all tell stories." Dietz reached out and

lifted a pastry from the salver. "I'm only interested in rewards. Gems, precious metals, things
of price. The Temple must be full of them. Think
of all the pilgrims who make offerings. Over the
years they would fill a hundred rooms the size of
this."

"One would be enough for me." Sanchez leaned
back in his chair, smiling, a grimace without
humor. "A private arena, a stable of fighters, a
selected audience. Easy money, Earl, don't you
agree?"

"Is that what you want?"

"As a hobby, of course. Even a rich man must
have something to occupy his mind. With what I
get from the Temple I'll build the finest establishment ever seen. Inlaid chairs, a ring of precious metal, attendants all dressed in silk. The
epitome of luxury. The peak of fighting skill.
Surely you've dreamed of owning such a place,
Earl? Of being on the winning side for a change."

Ellen Contera said, "What makes you think
Earl is a loser?"

"Could Rauch buy anything else?" Sanchez met
her eyes. "We are all after the same thing. The
Temple has it and we are going to rob the Temple. Money with which to establish ourselves."

"Just walk in and take it, huh?" Ellen shrugged.
"You think it will be as easy as that? Even a fool
would know better."

"Are you calling me a fool?" Sanchez glared his
anger. "Are you?"

"Anyone's a fool who walks blind into a trap,"
snapped Dumarest. "And before loot can be spent
it has to be won."

"Meaning?"

"You've been in the arena. What happens when a fighter is convinced he's already won? That he's got it made. When all he can think about is the money he'll get and the woman he'll pick and the feast that's waiting. What would you call such a man?"

"A suicide." Sanchez puffed out his cheeks. "I get the point."

"Keep it in mind. That goes for all of you." Dumarest looked from one to the other. "We don't know what's in the Temple. It doesn't matter. First we have to get to it. Any ideas?"

Kroy Lauter led the explanations, jabbing a thick finger at the map he unrolled, moving it to illustrate points.

"Raniang's a hard world. One little better than a cinder. The Hsing-Tiede Consortium has an installation there but it's on the other side of the planet from the Temple. Pilgrims usually arrive in groups on chartered ships which land here." His finger jabbed. "Well away from the Temple and down in this depression. Pilgrims march toward the Temple and enter the complex here." Again his finger rapped the paper. "They are met and escorted by priests. After certain ceremonies they are led into the Temple proper."

"Which is where the hard part begins." Altini leaned over the map. "We can only guess as to what really lies inside."

"Why guess?" Dumarest glanced at Ellen. "Don't we have maps? Diagrams?"

"The best I could get," she admitted. "But—"

"Things change," said Altini quickly. "Walls

built or removed. New paths opened in different chambers. Traps set in the floor. Even the rituals can vary. Those guarding the treasure aren't fools and we can't be the first to want to rob them."

Dietz said, "No matter how things vary the basics remain the same. A thing I learned when young at my trade. To hunt down a man, to place him in the right position for the kill, to strike home and escape capture—all depends on established habit-patterns. Discover them and the victim is helpless."

"An assassin's philosophy," sneered Sanchez. "You are saying a man cooperates in his own murder."

"Unconsciously, yes. As you may easily cooperate in your own defeat when—"

"Nonsense!"

"No," said Dumarest. "A fighter, any fighter, can't help but follow a certain pattern. He will repeat winning maneuvers, hold his blade in a familiar way, stand in a workable position. Watch him long enough and you can plan his defeat." He changed the subject; if he had to fight Sanchez then the less he knew the better. To the assassin he said, "You were talking about the basics, Pinal. Would you please continue?"

He listened, checking points, evaluating available data. Too little was based on known fact, too must rested on assumption. Yet it was logical to expect that the treasure, whatever it was, would remain in its shrine. That ceremonies would remain basically unaltered. That Karlene, despite her conditioning, would have yielded essential data as to the interior of the Temple.

He remembered how Altini had cut Ellen short and wondered at his reason. Later, when the discussion was over and the others had drifted apart, he spoke of it to her as they walked beside the garden wall.

"Ahmed is a thief and as such he tends to be cautious. Also he is proud and wants to enhance his prowess."

"Is that all?"

"Of course." She turned to look at him, smiling. "What other reason could there be? You can trust him, Earl."

A conviction Dumarest didn't share. He said, "Are you coming with us?"

"Yes."

"I meant into the Temple."

"I can't do that." She walked seven paces in silence then added, "Remember we talked of weaknesses? Mine is pain. I can't stand it. I found that out on Kampher when some people I knew staged a rebellion. I didn't take part but I was taken in for questioning. They weren't gentle." She lifted her hands so as to display the livid blotches. "I told them everything they wanted to know."

"You can't be blamed for that."

"You are kind to say so. Not everyone would be so understanding. But I dare not go into the Temple and risk discovery by the priests. I learned from Karlene what will happen."

"Bad?" As she nodded, Dumarest added, "Is that the real reason Ahmed stopped you? Was he afraid you'd tell us what we'd face if we were caught?"

"Possibly. But, as I said, he can be trusted."

As the assassin, the fighter, the mercenary—all trusted to be hungry to make their fortunes. All united by greed. Not the best of motivations.

Ellen said, as if reading his thoughts, "Rauch had to take what he could get, Earl. That's why he wants you to take command."

Dumarest said, dryly, "Because I've guts, courage and intelligence?"

"You've got all that," she admitted. "But so have the others. What makes you special is that you have something else. A greater motivation." Halting, she turned to face him, to look up into his eyes. "They just want loot—but you want to find a world."

The air of Driest was far more salubrious than that of Erkalt and, instead of snow and ice, the window gave a view of rolling plains and distant hills all covered in a rich brown and green. A difference Clarge noted and dismissed as unimportant as he had the comfort of the room, the furnishings, the cool air vented through decorated grills. The room, the planet meant nothing.

Dumarest was gone.

The data lay before him: a mass of facts, reports, observations—the results of time-consuming but essential verification of statements made by those willing to help the Cyclan.

Again he checked them, feeling the mental glow of achievement which was the only real pleasure he could ever experience. His prediction had been correct—finding the woman had guided him to the man. Had he arrived a week earlier the hunt would now be over.

He rose from the desk, banishing thought of what might have been. To speculate in such a manner was a waste of mental direction and as useless as regretting the past. And all was not lost; when Dumarest had moved on he had not gone alone.

Mentally he reviewed the data he had obtained. An agent of Rauch Ishikari had chartered a vessel, the *Argonne,* and none knew where it was bound. Dumarest and the woman had resided with Ishikari. Investigation had shown they no longer occupied their quarters. A party had left in the chartered ship; a score of persons all muffled in masking robes but one of them, caught in a sudden gust of wind, had revealed a mass of shimmering white hair.

A genuine mistake or a deliberate diversion? A moment of accident or a false clue planted to lead any followers astray?

The former, he decided, the woman had left on the ship.

But where would it land?

Dumarest was on it; Clarge set the probability as high as 99.9 percent. As near as any cyber would go to predicting certainty. The woman also—but why was he still with her? What had she to offer?

The acolyte came at his signal, bowed as Clarge said, "Total seal."

Within his own quarters Clarge lay supine on the bed. A touch activated the wide band circling his left wrist, the device ensuring that no electronic scanner could focus on his vicinity. Relaxing, he closed his eyes and concentrated on the Samatchazi formulae. Gradually he lost the use of his senses; had he opened his eyes he would have been blind. Locked within his skull his brain ceased to be irritated by external stimuli. It became a thing of pure intellect, its reasoning awareness its only connection with normal life. Only then did the grafted Homochon elements become active. Rapport followed.

Clarge blossomed into a new dimension of existence.

Each cyber had a different experience. For him it was as if he were a point of expanding parameters; rings which widened to the end of the universe, renewed and replenished by further rings. A point which pulsed and moved through realms of scintillating brilliance, connecting, interchanging, embracing everything in a composite whole. The living part of an organism which had transcended the limitations of flesh and moved with the freedom of unrestricted thought.

And all was rooted in the heart of the Cyclan.

Buried deep beneath layers of adamantine stone Central Intelligence absorbed his knowledge as a sponge soaked up water. Mental communication, almost instantaneous, made him one with the massed brains.

Information given and orders received—but this time Clarge wanted more.

"Check on the origins of a tattoo." He described it in detail; information gained from Hagen. "Worn on the region above the left breast."

A question.

"The woman, Karlene vol Diajiro."

A query.

"Dumarest is with her. She must be leading him. The tattoo could provide the answer to where."

A command.

Clarge waited as Central Intelligence searched the massed intelligence which made it what it was. Brains removed from the skulls of cybers who had earned the reward of near-immortality, lying still alive and aware in sealed vats of nutrient fluid, all hooked in series with each other to form a composite whole. An ideal state in which to ponder the problems of the universe. A combination which formed a tremendous organic computer of incredible complexity working to establish the rule and dominance of the Cyclan.

Once, perhaps centuries ago, a cyber had seen or learned of the tattoo. Or had been told about it when an acolyte. A memory which, like all memories, would never die. Now, stimulated by need, it woke to provide the answer.

Clarge spun in an intoxication unsurpassed by any drug. A mental euphoria in which he sensed strange memories and alien situations—the scraps and overflow of other minds. The residue of other intelligences. A stimulation which always followed rapport but was now enhanced by an added dimension. One which would ensure his reward.

Clarge opened his eyes, waiting until the ceiling grew clear and small sounds adopted meaning. Always it took time for the workings of the body to become realigned with the dictates of the mind. He swayed a little as he rose from the bed and sat again knowing he had been too impatient. A fall now would demonstrate his inefficiency; minutes were not important now that he knew where Dumarest was heading.

Chapter 9

Raniang was worse than Lauter had described: a cinder scoured by abrasive winds, the air acrid with chemical taints, the whole lit by a sullen red giant which tinged everything with the color of blood. Lying prone on a crest, head and body masked by massive boulders, Dumarest stared through binoculars at the Temple below.

It was uncannily familiar; Ellen had done a good job of interpreting Karlene's memories in order to build her model. Rugged walls enclosed open spaces with openings in a complex pattern which would trap the unknowing in a maze. The central dome, the squat towers, the flanking buildings all looked the same but the basic mystery remained. The inner part of the Temple was still an unknown quantity.

"Earl?" The voice came from the speaker in his ear. Altini's voice. "Anything new?"

"No." Dumarest sub-vocalized, the vibrations of his larynx transmitted by the throat-mike. "They're still in there."

A party of twelve all muffled in black robes who had wended their way from the landing field. Robed priests had met them at the entrance to the external complex and had guided them through the labyrinth. A path Dumarest had memorized but, even as he watched, laboring figures were busy blocking some openings and creating others. Windblown dust would form a patina over the alterations and make a mock of any memorized path.

"Neat," said the thief when Dumarest transmitted the information. "Enter one way and leave by another and both will be changed before the next party of worshipers arrives. I'll bet they operate the same way inside. Earl, see—"

"Wait!" Dumarest adjusted the binoculars. "They're coming out."

Wind gusted, blurring the view, but he could see the small column as it wended its way from the heart of the complex. The devotees wore black robes devoid of any insignia or decoration. Those worn by the priests, also black, bore a stylized sunburst on breast and back. Dumarest counted, frowned, counted again as the column crossed an open space.

Altini said, as he reported, "Two short? Are you certain?"

"Fifteen went in: the party and three priests. Thirteen are coming out. Three of them are priests." He waited as the column reached the outer wall and separated into two groups. "Ten heading back to the landing field."

"But—"

"Cut it!"

The radio operated on a scrambled frequency, but an electronic ear could pick up the noise and a monitoring guard could become suspicious. If the Temple had electronic ears and guards on watch—but Dumarest, willing to take a small risk, was reluctant to take unnecessary chances. Now he slipped the binoculars back into their case and began to ease himself back from the crest. Dirt scraped harshly beneath his stomach and chest, a gritty, rasping sound, that was repeated as he drew free of the sheltering boulders.

Nightmare reared from the dirt inches before his face.

It was black, spined, edged with hooked and spindled legs. An insect, two feet from barbed tail to gaping mandibles. Curved and serrated arcs of shearing destruction. They swung toward his throat as acid sprayed at his eyes.

The acid caught his cheek, the jaws closing on his left arm as Dumarest threw himself sideways to roll on the dirt. As the barbed tail slammed against his chest he tore the knife from his boot and sent the razor-sharp edge to slash at the segmented body. As the swollen abdomen fell he thrust the point between his sleeve and a mandible, twisted, heaved, the broken jaws joining the rest of the body.

The body eaten even as he climbed to his feet by other nightmare shapes; predators who lurked in the dirt, attracted to their prey by the vibrations of movement, the scent of flesh and water.

Ellen Contera pursed her lips as she examined Dumarest's cheek.

"Nasty. If it had hit your eyes you'd be blind now. Here." A spray took away the pain. Another sealed the raw patch beneath a transparent dressings. "Anything else?"

"No." The mesh beneath the plastic of his clothing had saved him from all but bruises. "Why didn't Karlene mention the local wild life?"

"She probably never saw any or, if she did, she was told they were other than dangerous. Pets, maybe." Ellen shrugged. "Is it important?"

"It stops us hanging around."

Dumarest stepped from the woman's cabin into the passage. The *Argonne* was small; a ship little larger than a rich man's pleasure craft, but the engines were good enough to have carried them into the Sharret Cluster and strong enough to have beaten the hazards always present in such a conglomeration of suns. An expensive vessel to operate and far from cheap to charter. Dumarest wondered just how far Ishikari was willing to go to chase his dream.

He sat with the others in the salon, old, withered, only his eyes truly alive.

As Dumarest entered the compartment he said, "Are you certain about the diminished party?"

"Yes."

"How do you account for it?"

Dumarest looked at the man, saying nothing.

He had traveled fifty miles by raft back to where the ship rested in a shallow valley. But for his natural quickness he would be blind now, dead.

Altini said, quickly, "Some wine, Earl? You look as if you could use it. How bad was the thing which attacked you?"

"Bad enough." Dumarest took the goblet the thief handed him. "The predators limit our course of action. We can't make camp and wait and watch until we pick the right time. I wasn't too keen on doing that anyway—the longer we hang around the greater the chance they'll discover us."

"If they do we'll be staked out on the dirt." Lauter rubbed at his chin. "I still think a frontal attack is the best policy."

"A hundred men," said Sanchez dryly. "Lasers, gas, heavy weapons. Explosives to smash down walls. Attack the Temple as you would a fortress. Well, I guess it would work, given enough men and had the money to pay for them." He glanced at Ishikari. "Or could swear there was enough loot to compensate for their time, trouble, dead companions and wounds. Of course, if there wasn't, they wouldn't be gentle."

Dietz said, "Those in the Temple must have friends. My guess is that any frontal attack would be crushed before it got very far. The Hsing-Tiede Consortium," he explained. "It has to be more than it seems."

"Which leaves us where?" Altini poured himself more wine. "Earl?"

"We head for space," said Dumarest. "Wait for a ship to arrive with worshipers. We follow them down and join their party." He lifted a hand to still any protest. "If we come in alone we'll be too small a group to get by. If we hang around waiting for a party and then try to join it we could be noticed and, anyway, the predators don't make that a good idea."

"We could drive a shaft into the dirt," said Ellen. "Rig a motor to give vibration. It would draw the pests to it."

"Some yes," admitted Dumarest. "But we can't move around without causing vibration; our footsteps, the beat of our hearts, the pulse of our blood. And why do things the hard way?"

"Land," mused the assassin. "Step out of the ship and catch up with the other party. Mingle with them until we're in the Temple. Learn what we can and then—" His hand made a chopping motion. "We may need to make a speedy retreat."

"The raft can provide it." Dumarest rose to his feet. "I'll work out the details later."

He was tired, the wound beginning to burn again and he guessed the acid must have contained a soporific of some kind. The edge of the salon door hit his shoulder as he left the compartment and twice he staggered and almost fell. A door opened beneath his touch and he caught the scent of perfume, saw the muted sheen of silver in softly diffused lighting.

"Earl!" Karlene came toward him, embraced him, held him close. "Darling! I'm so afraid!"

"It was nothing." He reassured her as he stroked her hair. Against his body he felt the faint quivering of her flesh. "Barely a scratch, see?" He tilted his head to display the wound on his cheek then noticed the blank stare of her eyes. "Karlene?"

She made no response and he guessed she hadn't heard him. Guessed, too, that her fear wasn't for him but stemmed from something far deeper. The working of her talent which had made this world a living hell. The world and the Temple which had been her home.

"Karlene!"

She moaned like an animal in pain, one lost and helpless and unable even to run. Cringing in his arms, her eyes glazed, little bubbles frothing the corners of her mouth. The sting of his hand barred her cheek with livid welts.

"Karlene! Karlene, damn you! Snap out of it!"

Crude therapy but it worked. The glaze left her eyes and she straightened a little, the tip of her tongue destroying the foam on her lips.

"Earl!" Her hands clutched at his neck, his shoulders, "The scent, Earl. So strong. God, so strong!"

Death and terror lying in the future, waiting to pounce, to become real.

"Be calm, darling." His hand soothed her hair, her body. "You're safe now. Just relax. Take deep breaths and relax. Relax."

Loosen the muscles and slow the pounding of the heart. Let the nerves unwind and the screaming tension dissolve. Ignore the threat of the future in the comfort of the present. Relax and sleep. Sleep.

But, later, when the captain had lifted the

Argonne into space, she jerked and writhed in his arms as she threshed in the nightmare of her dreams.

The robes were thin, cheap, black, cowling faces, concealing bodies, their hems trailing the ground. Copies of those worn by the worshipers Dumarest had watched and the uniform of those moving ahead. A score of pilgrims vented from the bowels of a battered vessel bearing indecipherable markings. Barely had they embarked when the *Argonne* landed to discharge its own load. Now the gap between the parties was closing.

Dumarest glanced back at the valley and the ships it contained. They stood wide apart, each a locked and isolated fortress, and he admired the captain's skill in handling his vessel. Before him rose the slope broken at the crest with undulating mounds like worn and fretted teeth. Those in the van ahead had reached it and were moving sideways as they followed an as yet invisible path.

Lunging forward Dumarest lessened the gap, the others following. There was no need of conversation; the plan and details had been worked out while waiting in space. Now, as he joined up with the major party, Dumarest stumbled, almost fell, caught at the arm of a man to regain his balance.

"Steady!" The man was middle-aged, soft beneath his robe, his face round and bland in the frame of his cowl. "This is no time to get hurt."

"Sorry." Dumarest straightened. "I guess I must have twisted my foot. I hope that's all it is."

"Lean on me if you want." The offer came without hesitation. "Each should share another's burden."

"As each should lighten another's path." Scraps of ritual learned from Karlene. Dumarest tested his weight, grunted, kept pace with the other as he moved on. "Have you been here before?"

"Twice." Pride edged the man's voice. "Your first time? I thought so. In a way I envy you—there can only ever be one first time. But this will be my last." He paused as if waiting for an expected response. One Dumarest didn't know. Instead he coughed, doubled, kept coughing, finally straightening to wipe his mouth. "Bad," said the man at his side. "With me it's cancer. In the stomach, early as yet but there's no point in waiting. In a way it's a relief. Now I don't have to make a decision—just serve the Temple for as long as I'm able."

The man stayed behind when the others left—had the two who had stayed earlier also been diseased? Was this the way the worshipers chose to end their days? But what care could they hope to get in the Temple?

Dumarest looked around. The path wended between soaring mounds, dipping, rising but never leaving the flanking shelter of dirt and stone. The others had forged ahead to mingle with the main party and he saw Altini walking close to a slender shape which could have been a woman. A suspicion verified as she turned to display her face—old, drawn, ravaged by time.

"Pollonia," said his companion. He had noticed Dumarest's interest. "She's staying too."

"Have you known her long?"

"We met on the ship. She joined it late."

He didn't say where and Dumarest didn't ask. It was enough to learn that the main party were mostly strangers to each other. A hurdle passed— but there would be others.

Dumarest left his companion as the line began to straggle, moving ahead, spotting the others. As the path finally left the shelter of stone and dirt and began to descend the slope toward the Temple the thief fell into step beside him.

"There's a grip," said Altini, his voice low. "A recognition sign. Give me your hand." His fingers gripped, pressed. "That's the question. Now for the response." Again his fingers pressed but this time in a different pattern. "Got it?"

"Have the others?"

"They will. Once more, now, just to make sure."

His fingers gripped and then he was gone to give the others the secret he had stolen. Before them waited priests, seven of them, tall, enigmatic in their robes, the sunburst insignia bright in the light of the scarlet sun.

"You are welcome."

Dumarest looked at the priest who had come to stand before him. Watched as a man went forward, knelt, hands lifted as if in supplication. As he rose to move toward an opening, Dumarest took his place.

"You are welcome."

Hands took his own; he felt the wide-spaced fingers press, linger until Dumarest returned the signal. Rising he followed the others to the opening, stood waiting as all were greeted, all tested.

"So far so good." Sanchez breathed the words,

not looking at Dumarest, his cowled face pointed toward the Temple. "What now?"

"We are friends. We traveled together. It would be suspicious if we acted as if we didn't know each other." Dumarest kept irritation from his voice—some men found it hard to remember simple instructions. "Just act as if you were genuinely what you claim to be."

A pilgrim, one a little overawed, more than a little overwhelmed by the majestic expanse of the Temple. A man enamored yet constrained by respect. One who couldn't help but show his interest but one who wouldn't stare for too long.

A role Dumarest acted as the priests guided them through the maze. A long, convoluted journey which ended at the massive walls of the central complex. Great doors decorated with abstract designs stood open beneath overhanging eaves, then closed behind them with the sonorous throb of a beaten drum.

"Welcome to the Temple of Cerevox."

The priest was tall, old, thin within his robe, adorned not with the sunburst insignia but a design composed of interconnected circles. Staring at it Dumarest was reminded of the Seal of the Cyclan and looked to where the pattern was repeated on the altar at which the priest stood. A block of stone as black as night set on a raised platform so as to dominate the entrance hall. Flames from flambeaux set to either side threw a dancing, ruby sheen over those assembled.

"For time beyond the count of mortals has the truth here being guarded. From the very first, when those bearing the fruit of true knowledge settled and dedicated their lives to the preservation of the heritage of Man, has the Original Secret resided within these walls. Only those who share our heritage may enter this place. Only those who are true in heart, in mind and spirit, may unite with us here in harmony."

Like the priest, the voice was old but, again like the speaker, it held the strength of burning conviction. The voice of a fanatic.

Those answering it were like the dry rustle of leaves.

"All praise to the Guardians."

"Here, now, the past and the present are one!"

"As it was so let it be."

"Let your hearts be humble!"

"We grovel in the dirt at the feet of truth." A concerted movement and the floor was covered with the black-robed bodies of the worshipers. "We are blinded by the light of revelation."

The introductory ceremony, at least, presented no problems. Dumarest mouthed as if making the correct responses, bowing, lying prone as he darted glances to either side. The walls appeared solid. The roof was heavily groined with carved supports of inset pillars. Dimly, in the flaring light of the flambeaux, he could see the shapes of attendant priests. They bore touches of scarlet on their robes. A higher rank, he guessed, or those who were entrusted to do the bloody work of executioners. Speculation ended as the old priest fell silent, stepping back as, in a line, the worshipers moved past the altar to make their donations.

"For the Temple." A woman, not Pollonia,

tipped a bag and let gems fall like glinting rain on the black stone. "May it stand always as Guardian of the Truth."

"For the Temple." A man set down a small bar of precious metal.

Another had coins, thick, gemmed, easily negotiable wealth. He followed the others who had gone before to stand at a door flanked by priests. Beyond it, Dumarest guessed, would lie the inner precincts of the Temple, more ceremonies, a service of some kind, a view of sacred objects, incense, chanting, hypnotic repetitions. The basis of any ritual designed to reenforce obedience to authority.

The worshipers would be led like sheep, treated like sheep, herded the same way. To follow them would be to learn little.

"For the Temple."

More gems. More portable wealth. Dumarest glanced back at the line. Sanchez was closest; the assassin beyond him, Lauter, looming over a woman close to the end of the line. Altini, the thief, was last. For a moment their eyes met, then Dumarest turned away. Three others stood before him, one the man he had spoken to on the trail.

"For the Temple." He made his donation. Then, instead of moving on, he rested both arms on the altar. "I also dedicate my heart, my spirit, my body, my life. To be used as a bastion for the truth."

The priest said, "You choose a hard path."

"Willingly."

"The step is irrevocable."

"That I accept as I accept all things. Grant me the supreme joy of serving to the end of my days the truth which has dominated my existence."

After a moment the priest lifted a hand. "It is so granted."

Attendants led the man to one side, to where a door gaped in the wall, one set far from that before which the others waited.

"For the Temple."

A man made his donation.

"For the Temple."

Another did the same and Dumarest stepped forward to take his place. He coughed as he reached it, doubling as he had on the journey, straightening, the cowl falling back from his face.

"For the Temple." He set down the small bag containing items of jewelery. He followed it with both arms set on the stone. "I also dedicate my heart, my spirit, my body, my life. To be used as a bastion for the truth."

Ellen Contera said, "Earl dedicated himself? What the hell made him do that?"

Altini shrugged. He sat in the salon of the *Argonne,* his face marked with lines of fatigue. The wine he held did little to refresh him. Later there would be drugs but, for now, it was good just to sit and rest and savor the sweet comfort of the wine.

"And the others?" Ishikari was impatient. "What of them? Speak, man!"

"They followed Earl. A contingency plan."

Altini sipped at his wine. The *Argonne* was in space, drifting high above Raniang, the captain following his instructions. Karlene, drugged, was somnolent in her cabin. Far below, night had closed over the Temple. When it thickened he would return.

"Earl saw his chance and took it," explained the thief. "A way to get close to the heart of the Temple. Ordinary worshipers don't come close. Earl must have guessed that. He gave me the signal to stay out of it and went ahead. The others joined him. I followed the rest."

"Into the Temple?" Ellen leaned closer. "What did you see?"

"I'm not too sure."

"Try to remember. I could help you if you want."

"No." He smiled and lifted his glass. "I've had enough hypnotism. You were right about that: chanting, drums, flashes of light, repetition, ritual responses, movements, all of it. I dug my nails into my palms and managed to keep a clear head. It wasn't easy."

"But you managed." Ishikari gnawed at his lip. "But what did you see?"

A chamber reached by a sinuous passage decorated with a host of beasts and birds, reptiles and all manner of living things. A roof glistening with artificial stars. Priests chanting to either side, some with the scarlet insignia, others with the sunburst, few with the convoluted rings.

"No women?" Ellen fired the question. "No priestesses?"

Not in the passage but in the great hall to which it led nubile girls had offered small cups of pungent liquid which had to be swallowed at a gulp. Symbolic blood of a symbolic world, or so

Altini had guessed. He had managed to retain most of the fluid, spitting it out later when unobserved, but the little he had swallowed had made his ears buzz. As had the pound of music; the wail of pipes and the throb of drums. A beat designed to match that of his heart, to slow it, to weave about him a strange, almost mystic detachment, enhanced by the dancing of the girls, the directed movements of the worshipers. Before him a world had opened, strange, alien, brightly exciting. One which held a touch of fear.

"It was creepy," he said. "I can't describe it better than that. A feeling of danger."

Of danger and excitement as would be felt by a child exploring a reputedly haunted house. An adult teasing a serpent. One who yielded to the desire to test personal courage by risking an action which could destroy if followed too far.

And then came the climax of the ceremony.

"You saw it?" Ishikari was intent. "You saw what the Temple contains?"

"I don't know. A part of it, perhaps, but that's about all. It was—" Altini broke off, shaking his head. "It was—strange."

Objects set in cases encrusted with gems and precious metals. Things which the priests displayed as if they were sacred relics. Most had knelt and kissed the containers. Others had stood as if entranced. All had given their total attention to what they were shown. And then had come the climax.

"A light," said Altini. "A blue glow which seemed to pulse. One without heat."

"You saw it?"

"I saw something." The thief swallowed more wine, not looking at the old man. "A reflection, maybe. A glow seen through complex mirrors. I had that impression. I also felt that, if I had seen it direct, I would have lost my eyes."

"The living God shining in resplendent glory at the heart of the Temple," mused Ellen. "In the Holy of Holies. Is that what they said it was?"

"Not exactly. The hint was there, maybe, and some could have taken it for that. But they didn't talk of God. It was Earth, they said. Mother Earth."

"Which they worship. Anything else?"

"Not much. There was bowing and chanting, then the light vanished and it was over. The priests made gestures, a blessing of sorts, maybe, then we were led out." He added, "It seemed a hell of a long way back to the valley."

"Is that all?" Ishikari made no effort to mask his disappointment. "Damn it, man, you went—"

"I was doing a job." Altini finished his wine and slammed the goblet hard on the table. "I wasn't there to enjoy the sights. You want to know just what happened? Every word spoken? Every gesture made? Then join the next batch of pilgrims. You might be lucky and get away with it. Then, when you come out, you'll have your answers."

But not all of them. Ellen said, quickly, "You're tired, Ahmed. Short-tempered and I can't blame you. Did you find out what you wanted to know?"

He was a thief and had noticed things others would have missed; the layout of the passage and chambers, nooks in which a man could hide, vents through which he could crawl. While the others had bowed, chanting, he had watched and studied; the twist of smoke in the air as it rose pluming from smoldering incense, the touch of subtle drafts, the echoes of shuffling feet, the set of shadows and the texture of walls and floor. A master of his trade who scented weakness like a dog scented blood.

Later, when he rested in his cabin, pipes feeding energy into his veins, metabolism speeded by the use of slowtime which stretched minutes into hours, Ellen returned to join Ishikari.

He sat, thoughtful, spinning an empty goblet in his fingers, small droplets of wine clinging to the interior, moving so as to trace elaborate patterns on the glass.

Without looking up he said, "Will he be ready in time?"

"I've given him forty hours subjective. He'll wake hungry but fit." She added, "By the time he's eaten and aligned himself it'll be two hours from now."

"The moon sets in three." It was barely a crescent but a little light was more dangerous than none. "He'll have plenty of time."

"Plenty," she agreed. On Raniang the nights were long. "It'll work out."

"Maybe." Ishikari turned the goblet again then blinked as, without warning, the stem shattered in his hands. "Earl," he said. "Why—"

"Did he split his forces?" She shrugged, impatient with his lack of understanding. "A wise move. He and the others on the inside and Altini free to operate on the outside. Who better than a thief to break into the Temple? If Earl makes a distraction he could make his way to the inner chambers. Or it could be the other way about. I'm not worried about that."

"Then what?"

"The glow," she said. "The mystic chanting. The worship of a God-like something. The way some pilgrims offer themselves to the Temple. And the way Karlene's acted ever since we arrived here. Her terror. That's why I've kept her drugged. The thing which made her run in the first place is tearing at her mind. The foreknowledge of death and fear—and it's so strong, so close."

He looked up, ignoring the broken glass, the blood which welled from a tiny wound on a finger to form a ruby smear.

"What has that to do with us?"

"Religions change," she said. "Like all institutions. What begins as one thing ends as another. Sometimes circumstances dictate the change, sometimes expediency. In times of stress it can be the worshipers themselves. They need to take a greater part, to bind themselves closer to the object of their veneration and, always, the priests will accommodate them. Those who serve a god serve the greatest power they can imagine. They share in that power. And the more demanding their god the greater it becomes. Maybe the Temple has passed the line."

She saw he didn't understand.

"Donations," she explained. "Personal attachment. The binding of the young to serve. But it

needn't stop there. The line between symbolism
and reality can be passed. When that happens
token surrender isn't enough." Pausing she added,
"I think Earl could have offered himself for
sacrifice."

Chapter 10

The man with cancer was Nakam Stura, a merchant, he explained and, from his clothing, Dumarest guessed he had been successful. The robe covered soft fabrics of expensive weaves and he wondered why the man hadn't used his wealth to buy medical treatment.

"We all follow the Wheel." Stura answered his unspoken question. "The Mother knows what is best. To fight against what is to be is to act the child. Better to accept with dignity and to serve as one is able. As you chose to do, my friend. As Pollonia and Reigan. In submission lies contentment."

They waited in a room to which a priest had guided them. One with bare stone walls and a floor of tessellated segments of black and amber. Light shone from sources beyond tinted panes: a luminous glow enhanced by the minute flames of

vigil lights set before various places on the walls.
Reigen knelt before one, hands clasped, head lowered, words a soft mumble as he prayed before
the stylized depiction of a quartered circle. A
man like the woman, old, drawn, his face ravaged by time. One with eyes lost in a vision of
things Dumarest couldn't discern.

"He lives only for the Mother," said Stura.
"Always he has longed for her embrace."

As had they all—if they were what they purported to be.

Dumarest edged away, sensing danger, not
knowing when a word or remark would reveal
him for what he was. Lauter, big, solemn, sat to
one side, his face blank, eyes glazed as if lost in a
world of his own. Dietz, small, restless, paced to
one side. He slowed as he caught Dumarest's eye
and turned to concentrate on a vigil light, the
round, blotched circle it illuminated.

Sanchez said, softly, "How long are we supposed to wait here?"

He had drifted close and spoke without looking
at Dumarest but, even so, he was being unwise.
As he had been willful when dedicating himself
to the Temple. He should have followed Altini;
instead, greed for loot had made him ignore the
plan.

Now he said, "We could break out. Grab a few
of the priests and find out what they know. Gather
what we can and get on with what we came to do."

Dumarest said, "The Mother is merciful."

"What?"

"If you have sinned then there will be forgiveness."

"Earl—"

"Be patient." Dumarest glanced at the ceiling, the tinted panes, the frieze cut into the wall of the chamber. Who knew who could be watching? Listening to every word? In a whisper he added, "Act the part you chose to play. Settle down. Pray. Look blank and wait. Damn you, wait!"

Beyond the chamber there would be ceremonies under way. Priests busy with the function of the Temple. The worshipers who would leave needed to be attended to—those who had dedicated themselves could be left for a time. He sat, hearing the soft mumble of Reigan's voice. Pollonia sighing as she sat in an apparent trance. Even the merchant was silent, head lowered, chin resting on his chest.

What would happen if he should change his mind and buy the treatment which would save his life?

A question Dumarest knew he dare not ask. He leaned back, shoulders against the wall, forcing himself to relax as he had done so often before when waiting to enter the arena. He drifted into a calming detachment during which his powers were conserved and vital energies husbanded.

In his mind he saw the model of the Temple, the plans of its interior. Guesses, but better than nothing and, so far, they had confirmed Karlene's memory. The great entrance doors, the altar, the passage which must have lain beyond, the one they had followed to this room—a chamber set on a lower level; others would adjoin it. Halls, more chambers, more passages. Places where she had worked and others where those serving the Tem-

ple had eaten, cooked, slept. A lot of people, a lot
of rooms—but still the inner chambers posed a
mystery.

How long had it been?

Dumarest glanced at the chronometer strapped
to his wrist; an instrument which was more than
it seemed. Time had moved faster than he had
guessed and he inhaled, filling his lungs with air
drawn through his nose, catching a pungent sweet-
ness, a hint of acridity. Incense and something
else, a truth-inducing vapor of some kind, perhaps, if they were under test it would be natural.

Lauter must have scented it too. He rumbled
and sat upright and snorted as if to clear his nose.
Rising, he crossed the room and checked the door.
It resisted his pressure.

To Dumarest he whispered, "I don't like this.
We're in a cage. The air stinks and I've the feeling trouble's on its way."

"So?"

"Why wait for it? We've got to do something."

Dumarest said, softly, "Use your head, man.
We're outnumbered by the priests. We don't know
where the treasure lies. We don't even know the
way out and, even if we did, where would we go?"

"But—"

"They have to make the first move. Until then
we wait." He added, "And watch Sanchez. He's as
jumpy as you are."

As Dietz could be but, if so, he didn't show it. A
gambler who had learned to mask his features.
An assassin who knew that he could be his own
worst enemy. He glanced at Dumarest as if about

to speak, then changed his mind as the door swung open.

Girls like angels stepped into the room.

They were young, lithe, nubile, neatly dressed in gowns which fell to just below the knee. Each had the left shoulder bared and on the soft flesh the imprint of a tattoo shone in reflected splendor. Each bore a tray on which rested a bowl, a plate, a steaming cup.

"Food." Sanchez smiled at the girl who proffered him her tray. "At least they aren't going to starve us. And what of you, my dear? Are you also a gift of the Mother?"

A fool, careless with his tongue, Dumarest saw the stiffening of Stura's face, the expression in Pollonia's eyes. Only Reigan, lost in his private world, seemed not to have noticed.

"All things are gifts of the Mother." The girl lifted her tray. "Eat so as to gain strength to serve her."

"And after?"

"Eat!" Dumarest took the tray from the girl and thrust it into the fighter's hands. To the girl he said, "How long must we wait before we can serve?"

"The ceremonies are almost over. When the worshipers have left, the priests will come for you." Her hand reached out and rested on his own. "You are strong and that is good. You must stay strong for the Mother needs you. Now eat and be patient."

The bowl held a thin stew composed of stringy fibers which could have been meat together with an assortment of vegetables. The plate bore a portion of hard, dark, gritty bread. The cup held hot water into which herbs had been infused.

"Today is a special day," said the girl who had given Dumarest his tray. "And so we eat the feast of celebration."

"Will you share it with me?" He read the answer in her eyes. "Here."

He watched as she spooned up the stew and dug sharp teeth into the bread. Not drugged, then, or if it was she didn't know it. And there was no mistaking her pleasure. He remembered what Ellen Contera had told him and wondered if the girl thought she was eating rare and expensive viands, drinking fine and special wine.

"Where will the priests take us?" Dumarest smiled as she stared at him. "After the meal," he urged. "Where will we go?"

"Down toward the inner chambers."

"And?" As she didn't answer, he said, "Do all those who dedicate themselves to the Temple go down to the inner chambers?"

"Of course. The old and flawed and those who are ill." She glanced at Pollonia. "Those who seek comfort and to rest. And the strong." Her eyes met his own. "Those who are not young."

"What is down there?" He saw the sudden blankness of her eyes. "Do you know? Can you tell me?" Then, quickly, knowing he had pressed too hard, he said, "Forget it, my dear. Just finish the wine."

It was night before the priests came. Five of them, tall, their robes adorned with the sigils of convoluted circles. The eldest, a man with a face ravaged with pits and lines, stared at them with deep-set, burning eyes. A fanatic who strode from one to the other as if reading their secret thoughts. The woman he ignored as he did Reigan who was still on his knees.

To Nakam Stura he snapped, "What ails you?" He nodded at the answer, turned to Dumarest. "You?"

"My lungs." Dumarest coughed and fought for breath. "A parasitical spore. I guess I haven't long to go."

"You?"

"I am fit," said Ramon Sanchez. "Strong and eager to serve."

Dietz whispered that he had an affliction of the heart. Lauter complained of his wounds.

"A laser burn in the gut," he explained. "Plates in both legs. A bullet still riding near my spine. I could get fixed, I suppose, but what's the point? I'd rather serve while I still have something to offer."

"You come from where?"

"Chalcot. I was a mercenary."

A mistake—the Original People did not follow paths of violence. Lauter had betrayed himself by volunteering his profession. Yet the priest made no comment and Dumarest wondered at his indifference as he led the way from the room down winding passages which fell in a spiraling decline beneath his feet.

A long journey ending in a gallery flanked with doors. Light blazed from the ceiling, a cold, blue luminescence which drained the natural color from flesh and left it the grim hue of lead.

"Later you will be given instruction," said the priest. "Now you will rest. You," his finger stabbed at the woman. "In there." The finger stabbed again as Pollonia moved toward a door. "You and you in there." He moved on as Reigan and Stura hastened to obey. At the end of the gallery stood wider doors, the air tainted with an acrid stench. "You in there and you," the finger pointed at Lauter, "in there."

A division Dumarest didn't like, for it had separated the false from the genuine and had split the mercenary from his companions. At his side Dietz murmured, "He spotted Kroy for a fake."

"Us too, maybe."

"Does it matter?" Sanchez looked up at the glowing ceiling, down at the room, the long row of cots it contained. "The priests are fools. They didn't even trouble to search us."

"What would you have done had they tried?"

"Fought, what else?"

"They could have guessed that. Why risk their skins when there is no need?" Dumarest looked at the nearest of the cots. "We don't seem to be alone."

A man lay on the fabric stretched on a frame. His face was mottled with sores as were his hands, his arms and naked torso. Ugly, oozing pustules which had stained the cot with crusted smears. He was asleep or drugged, moaning a little, a thin skein of white hair fringing the dome of his skull.

Another, not so badly afflicted, lay beyond him. A third lower down. As Dumarest walked along the cots a man reared toward the end of the room, turning his head, blinking eyes glazed with a nacreous film.

"Master? Is that you, Master? Am I again to serve the Mother?"

"Not yet," soothed Dumarest. He touched the man's naked shoulder. "Rest while you may and peace attend you in your dreams."

As they moved on, Sanchez said, softly, "They stink. They all stink of sickness and disease. Why the hell did the priests put us among them?"

"To serve."

"Not me. I'm no nurse."

Dietz said, patiently, "You do not understand, Ramon. We, they, are all of a kind. You heard the blind man. He yearns to serve. He must have offered himself for that." Pausing he added, "Just as we did."

To be used as the needs of the Temple demanded offering their hearts, spirits, lives, bodies. Dumarest remembered the meal, the thin stew with the stringy shreds of meat. The Temple was on a harsh world and those running it could not afford to indulge in the luxury of waste. Those dedicating themselves would be used to the full and, even when dead, they would still be of value.

He strode down the length of the room, counting the sick, the empty cots. About half and half which, if some were now working, explained the apparent carelessness of the priests. Labor was in short supply, especially the kind which was provided by those on the cots, and soon he and the others would be swallowed among them.

"It's crazy," said Sanchez. "If they suspect us why leave us free?"

"They suspect Kroy," said Dumarest. "We were separated from the others because we are more fit. But they don't know we arrived as a group."

"Are they stupid?"

"No," said Dietz. The assassin knew the strength of the established habit-patterns better than most. Knew too the encysting effect of established authority. He said, "We're operating on momentum. They take us for what we claim to be. We'll get by if we don't draw attention to ourselves as Kroy did."

"Or unless he betrays us." Sanchez looked at the door, scowling. "They could be working on him now. Coming for us at this very moment. I say we move."

"When they come for us," said Dumarest.

"Now."

"No. We wait."

"Like hell!" Sanchez strode toward the door, halted as Dumarest stepped before him. His teeth shone white between his snarling lips. "Get out of my way, damn you. Shift or—"

Dumarest moved, his left hand darting forward, catching the fighter's right forearm, jerking it from his body, the weapon he guessed the man was reaching for. His right hand stabbed forward and upward, fingers closing on the other's throat, fingers gouging deep to rest on the carotids.

"Relax," he said, coldly. "Kick or struggle and I'll close my hand." His fingers tightened in warning. Tightened more as Sanchez lifted his free hand. "Don't try it!"

"Don't!" Dietz was beside them. "Earl! Ramon! This is madness!"

Dumarest said, not looking at the assassin, "I agree, but so is running blind in the Temple. The place must be thick with priests. We could get some but the others would have us trapped. We must wait until they come for us. If necessary we'll defend ourselves but, if they've come to guide us, we play along." He eased the pressure on the fighter's throat. "I'm running this operation, Ramon. If you don't like it too bad. Do you play along or not?"

"I—" Sanchez swallowed as Dumarest lowered his hand. "You—"

"Forget the threats. I want an answer." He would get the answer he wanted or the fighter would lie dead on one of the cots. Sanchez recognized this. "Good." Dumarest glanced at his wrist as the man yielded. If the priests left them alone they would have to move but there was time yet. "Get some rest."

As Sanchez, smoldering with rage, moved to an empty cot Dumarest added, "That goes for you too, Pinal."

"You're a fool, Earl." Dietz spoke in a whisper. "Ramon will never forgive how you shamed him. You should have killed him. Give me the word and I'll do it for you."

"We can use him."

"Then, at least, give me the word." A different word, one which would free his mental restraints, and Dumarest wondered how the assassin knew he had been chained. "I tried," he explained, anticipating the question. "It wasn't hard to figure out how Ishikari had tricked me. Twice I tried to even the score. Twice I failed. The second time he told me why."

"Did you expect him to trust you?"

"He made me eat dirt," said Dietz bitterly. "Had me sweating with fear. But, worst of all, he trod on my pride." He looked at his hands, the minute quivering of his fingers. "He left me less than a man. I want to be whole again."

To use his skills, his drugs, his poisons, his trade. Hampered, he was safe but a tool which had lost its temper. A knife which had lost its edge. And no man should be a cripple.

Dumarest said the word.

And watched as a veil seemed to fall from the assassin's eyes. He straightened a little, breathing deep, the quiver now absent from his hands. A man as deadly as a serpent.

"Get some rest now," said Dumarest.

He felt the sting of the chronometer against his wrist as the man obeyed. Altini was on his way.

It was hard to move in the night. There was no moon but starlight cast a silver sheen and created deceptive shadows which masked stones and potholes and uneven footing. Terrain over which the thief raced with trained grace, sensing obstacles, avoiding them, moving on until he reached the outer complex of the Temple. His path was already plotted: not through the maze but over it. Dust gritted beneath the soft soles of his shoes as he ran along the tops of the walls, crouching, dropping to run over bare spaces, jumping gaps, moving like a flitting shadow toward the flanking buildings, the dome, the squat towers.

They would hold defenses, watchers, weapons to burn down unwanted rafts, to sear the bodies of any trying to gain unauthorized entry to the sacred precincts. Flattened against stone he studied them, the black grease on his face and neck merging with the color of the clothing he wore, the gloves hiding his hands. Carefully he lifted an arm, his fingers moving with the delicacy of spiders traversing shattered glass, pausing as they felt an invisible strand. An alarm, one he avoided as he climbed, a second he left behind him, a third which he neutralized with small instruments he took from a pouch at his waist.

Cracked stone provided easy holds and he rushed upward to move into the inward facing side of a tower, to freeze as he strained both eyes and ears.

He saw nothing but the loom of other towers, the silent barrenness of sloping roofs and the sweeping curve of the central dome. Were the towers deserted? He climbed higher and froze again at the sound of a shuffle, the drone of a voice.

It stilled, yielded to silence, commenced again as if it were a repetitive recording played on a machine. A routine prayer mumbled so often it had become as normal as breathing to the man on watch.

Altini climbed higher to where openings gaped in the stone toward the summit of the tower. Hanging by one hand he dipped the other into

his pouch, found a small cylinder, thrust his thumb
hard against an end and threw it into an opening.

He heard it hit, a startled exclamation, then
the sound of something heavy slumping to the
floor. One impact which meant a solitary guard
and he guessed the other towers would be as
sparsely manned. It was tempting to climb up
and into the tower. There would be a door of
sorts giving to the lower levels and access to the
main body of the Temple but to try that route
was to take too big a gamble. To maintain efficiency single guards would need frequent reliefs
and a change could be due at any time. It would
be safer to descend and cross the roofs in the
"blind" spot he had created. Shadows clustered
thick beneath the eaves and gave good cover.

Altini reached it, avoiding alarm wires and
pressure points which would have bathed the
roof in revealing light. Stone pierced with grills
ran beneath the eaves and he crouched beneath
one, sniffing, catching the heavy odor of incense.
Air vented from the hall below as he had suspected;
now he needed to find a way into the heart of the
Temple, the inner chambers where the loot would
be found.

Thieves' work and he was good at it. Like an
insect he moved from place to place, sniffing,
questing, careful of wires and traps. The openings in the towers were like blind eyes, the stars
distant, hostile, indifferent to sacrilege and the
impending rape of cossetted treasures. Soon now
he would have forced a way in, the Temple violated, the priests impotent in their power to protect their charge.

"Ahmed!" The voice whispered in his ear. Ellen's voice from where she waited with the raft. "Answer, damn you!"

"Trouble?" silently he moved his lips.

"Maybe. How are things going?"

"Well." He looked at the chronometer on his wrist. A twin to the one carried by Dumarest. "Is that what you called to ask about?"

"No. There's a raft heading your way. From the Hsing-Tiede Consortium, we think."

"Close?"

"Too close for comfort. It might be expected. Best to take cover."

"Out!"

Talking was dangerous in that it took concentration as well as time. Altini moved, eyes wary, feet and hands moving in neat precision. Grit made small, scratching sounds and something shifted to roll down the slope with a fading rattle. Broken stone or a shard of aged mortar but enough to betray him, and Altini tensed, his stomach tight to the anticipated challenge, the blaze of revealing light, the searing burn of a laser.

Then, abruptly, the raft was above him.

It rode high and straight, circling, bearing lights which flickered in a recognition pattern. It lowered, hovering, as searchlights bathed it. Lower until it passed the summits of the towers, the flanking buildings, to land in the outer complex close to the great doors. Watching, Altini could see the men it carried, the scarlet of the robe one of them wore.

Chapter 11

Dumarest rose from the cot as he felt the sting of the instrument on his wrist: Altini's signal warning that the thief was in position. Sanchez joined him as he headed toward the door, Dietz at his heels.

"We move?"

"Yes."

"Not before time." The fighter lacked patience. "What about Kroy?"

"We'll pick him up on the way." Dumarest looked at the cots, the men they contained. Already he'd made his choice. "Get the door while I collect a guide."

He was thin, ravaged, jerking awake at a touch, eyes wide as he saw the loom of Dumarest's body, the nighted color of his robe. A man confused, thinking he had been wakened by a priest.

"Get up," said Dumarest. "Come with me. I want you to show me where you work."

"I—"

"What is your name?"

"Ritter. Chang Ritter."

"Hurry, Chang. Come with me. The Mother commands it."

Sanchez was busy at the door. It was thick, heavy, fastened with a metal catch. It swung open beneath the fighter's hands and Dietz stepped into a passage, that was deserted and he led the way to the room where the mercenary had been taken. Dumarest heard him cry out as he entered.

"God! The swine!"

The room was small, holding only five cots, four of them empty, Lauter sprawled on the fifth. He was naked to the waist, his torso blotched with ugly wounds. Blackened rips as if hot pincers had torn at the flesh, charring tissue and releasing blood which had clotted to form carmine mounds.

"Kroy?" Dietz was at his side. "Kroy?"

Dumarest looked around. Water stood in a bucket on the floor and he lifted it, flung it over the mercenary where he lay. Before Lauter could move he was at his side, hand clamped over his mouth, nose closed by the pressure of thumb and finger. A hold which could kill but one which stimulated the mercenary's survival instinct. Lauter shuddered, heaved, lifted a hand to tear the constriction from his mouth.

"No noise," warned Dumarest. "Just take it easy."

Air made a rasping sound as Lauter filled his

lungs. He tried to sit upright, almost fell, made it as Deitz thrust an arm beneath his shoulders. For moments he could do nothing but sit and fight for breath then, as his tenacious grip on life asserted itself, he snorted, coughed, winced, as he swung his legs over the edge of the cot.

"What kept you?"

"Ask Earl." Sanchez glanced at Dumarest. "He made us wait."

"Just as well he did." Lauter looked at his chest. "Those bastards weren't gentle. They took me down the passage to a place they've got. Tied me up and had themselves some fun. Amateurs!" His contempt was real. "I could have had them spilling their guts in half the time."

"They questioned you?" Dumarest checked to see if Ritter was safe. "What did they want to know?"

"Who I was. Where I'd come from. Was I alone— stuff like that. I pretended I didn't know what they were talking about. When they put the irons to me I just yelled and slumped. I wonder you didn't hear me."

And lucky they hadn't. To have attempted a rescue would have been to join him in danger, as it was, the mercenary served to warn of what would happen if they were careless. As he straightened to his feet Dumarest studied the instrument on his wrist. Time was running out. Altini was on the roof. They had to find the secret the Temple contained, make their way upwards to the opening he would have made, join with him in the final run to safety.

A simple plan but one depending on speed. To

hit, to take, to run and, with luck, to do it before the alarm could be sounded.

"Let's get moving." Dumarest stepped toward the door, listened, thrust himself through the portal into the passage. It was still deserted and he stared at the guide. "Which way, Chang?"

Sanchez snarled as the man made a vague gesture. "The creep. Hasn't he any brains? I'll make him talk."

"You watch the rear." Dumarest was harsh. "You're too big with your mouth. I won't tell you again. Now, Chang, which way?"

Down the passage to a junction, to turn left, to follow a slope, to move through a door into another chamber. The cold, blue light ended, replaced by a warmer glow cast from scattered lanterns. Another passage swallowed them, the floor cracked and seemingly neglected, and Dumarest guessed it was used only for the passage of workers. Deeper into the maze of the Temple and he tensed to the sound of chanting.

"Kroy, drop back to stand beside Chang."

Dumarest moved to take his place as the mercenary obeyed. Himself and Dietz in the front, Sanchez at the rear, the two apparent workers in the middle. In the dimmer lighting they might just get by. Another gamble to add to the rest.

"Robes," whispered the assassin. "We need camouflage."

A need which grew as they progressed. The empty places were far behind now and more voices could be heard together with the rasp of sandals, the moving shadows which created soft rustlings. Even at night the Temple was busy.

"There." Dumarest halted as he heard Chang's voice. "No! Not on! There! There!"

He stood pointing at the wall, at a carving depicting a fanged and monstrous beast. His face was twisted as he stubbornly fought Lauter's dragging hand. A man like a machine which had been set in motion. One clinging to a familiar path.

Again his hand stabbed at the beast. "There!"

Dumarest said, "Is that the way the priests took you? Through the wall?"

"He's lying. It's solid." Lauter snorted his impatience. "You can see it is."

"Perhaps not." Dietz moved toward it, ran his hands over the carved stone, grunted as he felt a movement. "It's on a pivot. A secret door of some kind."

A convenience which enabled workers to attend their duties without encroaching on the devotions of those in adjoining chambers. Opened, it gave on to a narrow passage which led to a room stacked with brooms, cloths, jars of wax, other assorted materials. The passage continued to open in the well of an area brilliant with light.

"Hell!" Sanchez narrowed his eyes. "What's this?"

A door faced the one through which they emerged. It was set far back beneath an overhang and stood deep in massive blocks of stone. The symbol of the quartered circle was prominent over an ornate lock. To either side stairs led up to a gallery which swept in an arc to either side. Climbing them, Dumarest saw walls of polished stone heavily carved, the quartered circle predominent. Light shone from panels set into the roof. A clear, blue illumination which threw the troughlike bench running around the inner wall of the gallery into prominence.

From within it came the wink and flash of jewels.

"Loot!" Sanchez thrust himself forward. "This is it! This is what we came for!"

The donations of worshipers stored and accumulated over countless years. Rare books their covers crusted with gems, ornaments, necklaces, rings, torcs, bracelets, objects of intricate loveliness, the work of long-dead craftsmen, the valued treasures of generations set as votive offerings to what the Temple contained.

"Leave them!" Dumarest was sharp. "This isn't what we came for!"

The fighter ignored him. "Look at this?" Sanchez held a flower of metal, the petals composed of matching stones which glowed with ruby and emerald, sapphire and diamond. Precious metal beneath his fingers as he tore them from their settings. "And this!" A chalice of shimmering perfection. "And this!"

He ran down the gallery, caution forgotten, entranced by the treasure spread before him. A rapacious child snatching at scintillating toys, destroying them, thrusting handfuls of gems into his pockets.

"No!" Chang cried out in protest at the sacrilege. "Don't! Please don't!"

He ran forward, frail arms lifted in a hopeless attempt to stop the fighter. Sanchez turned, snarling, striking out with brutal force. Chang flew backward to hit against the edge of the trough, to slump like a broken doll, to lie on the polished stone of the floor, his head at a grotesque angle.

"No, Earl!" Lauter caught at Dumarest's arm. "He's mad. Crazed. Try to stop him and he'll kill you. I've seen it before. An entire squad. All they could see was loot."

And all Dumarest could see was the blood staining the dead man's mouth. A carmine smear which grew and grew until it filled the gallery, the entire universe.

There had been formalities which had added more time to that already lost but Clarge had had no choice but to yield to ancient tradition. Even while waiting for the ceremonies and rituals to end, his mind had been at work. The Temple was, to him, almost an open book. He could visualize what it must have been in the beginning; a shrine attended by dedicated attendants. One which had enlarged over the years, gaining status with bulk, stature from the donations of worshipers. Enhanced power and prestige would have accelerated the growth until the peak of optimum efficiency would have been reached and passed. Now revenue would have fallen, attendants fewer and of a lesser quality, those adhering to the creed it preached content to do so from afar, less inclined to make the arduous pilgrimage.

The way of all such institutions. Only the Cyclan would continue to grow and expand its influence over an endless succession of worlds. The secret domination which already controlled the destiny of a myriad planets and would lock

more into its expanding web. One day the entire
galaxy would be under that domination and then
there would be a final end to waste and stupidity.

Clarge could visualize it as he could the origins of the Temple in which he stood. It, like so
much else, would be swept away, the stones used
in its construction devoted to rearing buildings
dedicated to the pursuit of knowledge. Poverty
would end—able beings would be put to work,
fed, housed, maintained in a state of efficient
health, set to work to create the new way of life.
The whims of petty rulers would be abolished.
Emotional poisons eradicated. Birth, growth, death
and development controlled. Selected types bred
and genetic advantages incorporated into the human race. There would be no disease, no irration-
al loyalties, no catering to superstition. The mind
would be all. Logic, reason, intelligence, efficiency—the cornerstones of the new, bright and
glittering order to come.

The whisper of a gong brought him to full
concentration on the matter at hand. He stood
within the small room to which he had been
escorted, the hue of his robe warmly scarlet
against the dull brown of the walls, in sharp
contrast to that worn by the old man who came
toward him. But if his robe was black the insignia covering the breast was not. It glowed with
gems and precious metals, an elaborate sigil surrounding a quartered circle.

"My lord!" The cyber inclined his head. "I am
most honored that you have condescended to grant
me this audience. It is something you will never
have cause to regret. I would not have imposed

my presence in this sacred place but for the urgency of my mission."

Deference and polite words to a man who was little better than a superstition-ridden fool, but here, in the Temple, the High Priest held supreme power. A fact never to be forgotten if he hoped to enlist Varne's aid.

"Sit." A withered hand gestured toward a chair. As Clarge took it the High Priest dropped into another. "You are importunate, cyber."

"With reason. The need is great."

"Nothing is greater than the Mother." Varne waited as if expecting a comment. When none came he added, "Those who sent you assured me that you intend no harm. Did they lie?"

"They told the truth. I have come to make you an offer. I have cause to know that a man is interested in the Temple. He is not of your following. He would not hesitate to violate your sacred places. He—"

"That is impossible! The Mother would never permit it!"

"Yet—"

"No! The thought is sacrilege!"

To press the point would be to alienate the priest and Clarge recognized the danger. Recognized, too, the brittle situation he was in. Too much time had been wasted at the Hsing-Teide establishment before those in charge had even admitted the existence of the Temple. Then had come the tedious delay before permission had been granted for him to be received at the Temple. Time in which Dumarest could have come and gone—once again escaping the grasp of the Cyclan.

Clarge knew the penalty should he fail.

He said, "Have none appeared who are not what they claim to be?" He elaborated the question. "I am thinking of someone who seems unsure of the rituals. Who hesitates or avoids a direct response. He could pretend to be dumb or even blind. Or he could ask too many questions. Have you no check on those visiting the Temple?"

"The secrets of the Temple must remain inviolate."

"That is understood. But surely a stranger, pretending to be a pilgrim, would have been noticed? Or could be noticed?" Pausing, Clarge added, "If such a one should be discovered the Cyclan would pay well if he were to be handed into their charge. If you already have such a one I can assure you he will never be able to tell what he may have seen."

A bribe, a promise, trusted currency in all such negotiations and, despite his position, Varne was little different from any ruler intent on safeguarding his power. A hard, ruthless, ambitious man—none other could ever have achieved his eminence. Clarge was accustomed to the type: all that was needed was to guide him the way he wanted to go.

Varne said, "What is your interest in this man?"

"The Cyclan needs him."

"Which tells me nothing."

"Need more be told?" Clarge let the question hang, unwilling to say more yet knowing that the High Priest would demand it. "The man I am looking for is in possession of a secret stolen from the laboratories of the Cyclan. It is important that it be regained. Now, my lord, if we can come to some agreement?" He added, before the other could answer, "It is, of course, imperative that the man be handed over alive and unharmed."

"You add conditions to your demands?"

"Dead, the man will be useless," said Clarge. "Injured, his memory could be impaired. I demand nothing you are not prepared to give, my lord, but think of the advantages gained if you cooperate. The skill of the Cyclan at your disposal, advice and guidance as to investments, predictions as to the most probable outcome of events. Warnings as to hazards which might lie ahead."

"As you now warn of interlopers?" Varne's tone held irony. "It seems—" He broke off as a priest entered the chamber, stooping to whisper in his ear. Watching, Clarge saw the thin hand clench as it rested on the ebon robe.

As the man left, Clarge said, "News, my lord?"

Varne was terse. "You predict well, cyber. Men have violated the treasury. They were gassed and taken."

"Dumarest? Is one named Dumarest?"

"Perhaps." The High Priest rose from his chair. "Names are unimportant—all must die!"

Karlene woke, crying out, sitting upright in the bed, seeing on the bulkheads the fading traces of vanished dreams. Nightmares which had turned her drugged rest into a time of horror so that she clutched her knees and felt the thing in her mind coil and move like a writhing serpent, that left a trail of fear and terror.

Strong!

So close and strong!

"Karlene?" Ellen was at the opened door of the cabin. "Are you all right?"

She entered as the question remained unanswered, one hand reaching to brush aside the cascade of silver hair and rest on the pallid forehead, the other resting fingers on the slender wrist as she checked the pulse. Fast—Karlene's heart was racing and Ellen could feel the perspiration dewing the forehead.

"You were crying out," she said. "In your sleep. Did you have a nightmare?"

Karlene nodded.

"A bad one?" She was gently insistent on gaining an answer; talk, in this case, was good therapy. "Was it a bad one?"

"Yes."

"I thought so. Your heart is racing but that is to be expected. Temperature is high, too, but it will quickly fall. Why don't you take a shower? It will relax you."

"Later, perhaps." Karlene moved away from Ellen's hand. "Has there been any word?"

"From Earl? No. Not as yet but we didn't expect any, did we? Ahmed has the radio."

"From him then?"

"A routine report. He made it to the roof and was checking the structure for a suitable place to make an opening." Ellen was determinedly cheerful. "There's nothing to worry about. Everything is going to plan."

A lie, there had been no real plan, just opportunities seized as the chance occurred, but Karlene didn't question the statement. Instead she sat, staring at the bulkhead, eyes misted with introspection.

"I saw it," she said. "In my dream. Something terrible and bright. So very bright. It grew and grew and I tried to run from it but it grew too fast and I didn't seem able to move."

"A common dream." Perfume stood on a table beside the bed. Ellen reached for it, dabbed it on Karlene's temples, the hollow of her throat. "There's a psychological explanation for it but I won't bore you with it now. Just take my word for it that everyone has dreams like that. Just as they do about falling. You've had a dream about falling, haven't you? Of course you have. You wake up with a jerk, your heart pounding and all in a sweat as you did just now. But the dream doesn't mean anything. Dreams never do."

Her voice deepened a little as she applied more perfume.

"Why not relax now? You must still be tired. Just lie back and look at the ceiling. You don't have to close your eyes but there's no reason why you should keep them open. Yet the lids are so heavy. So very heavy. It would be much more comfortable to close them and sink into the soft, warm darkness. So very nice just to drift and think of pleasant things. To drift . . . to sleep . . . to sleep . . . to sleep . . ."

Hypnotic suggestion, a useful tool and one easy to use on a preconditioned subject. Ellen looked back at Karlene as she reached the cabin door hoping that the next time she woke she wouldn't fill the ship with the echo of her screams. It had been a mistake to bring her. She hadn't wanted to come. The Temple held too many unpleasant memories, but Ishikari had insisted and what he wanted he got.

Ishikari looked up from the table as she entered the salon, watching as she poured herself a drink, saying nothing until she had gulped it down.

"Is she settled?"

"Yes."

"Another dream?" He frowned at her nod. "I shouldn't have brought her with us but I didn't know she would react as she has. And we needed all the help we could get."

"We had all she could give."

"True, but I didn't know that. I thought she could act the part of a pilgrim, go into the Temple with the others, give them help and guidance."

"I would never have permitted that."

"No?" For a moment anger flared in his eyes then he shrugged. "Well, it can't be helped. Still nothing from Altini?"

"No."

"Why doesn't he keep in touch?" Ishikari pulled irritably at his chin. "He should make regular reports. He must know I want to keep abreast of what is going on."

"The radio was for emergency communications only." Ellen was patient, recognizing his anxiety, the strain he was under. "The mere fact we have heard nothing is a good sign. He may have decided against responding to our signals. He could be in a precarious situation. There could be monitors, anything. He wouldn't want to trigger an alarm." Suddenly she was tired of pandering to his conceit. "He's not fool enough to risk his neck just to satisfy your curiosity. You must trust his judgment."

A matter on which he had no choice. He rose from the table, pulling at his chin, a gesture she had never seen him make before. Once, perhaps, in years gone by, he had worn a beard and pressure had revived an old habit. Now he paced the salon, quivering, restless, a man yearning to grasp the concrete substance of a dream. One terrified lest the dream itself should vanish like a soap bubble in the sun.

"Relax," she said. "There's no point in wearing yourself out."

"It's getting late."

"It isn't that bad. Your time sense is distorted. It happens in times of stress. Here." She shook blue pills from a vial, handed them to him together with a glass of wine. "Get these down and you'll feel better." Her voice hardened as he hesitated. "Do it! I don't want another neurotic on my hands!"

And she didn't want to become one herself. She strode from the salon, feeling a sudden claustrophobia, a need for unrecycled air, the ability to stretch her vision. The *Argonne* had landed in a wide cleft to one side of a line running from the Temple to the Hsing-Tiede complex. Hills loomed to all sides making a framework for the night sky. One blazing with the stars of the Sharret Cluster. Suns which threw a diffused illumination over the area and created pools of mysterious shadow.

The crewman at the port killed the interior lights before opening the panel, catching at her arm as Ellen stepped to the edge.

"Careful. Don't get too close. There could be things out there."

Good advice and she took it, staying well back from the rim, looking up and breathing deep of the natural air. It caught at her throat and lungs with a metallic acridity and she was shocked then surprised that she had been shocked and then annoyed at herself for the conflicting emotions. The air was bad as was the planet, but the sky compensated for everything. A span of beauty graced with scintillant gems constructed of fire and lambent gases and swirling clouds of living plasma. The glory of the universe against which nothing could compete.

"My lady?" The crewman was anxious, eager to regain the safety of his sealed cocoon.

"All right." Ellen took a last breath of the acrid air. "You can close the port now."

She heard the clang as she headed toward the salon, back to the harsh metal of decks and bulkheads, the prison men had created to travel between the stars. Even as she walked her hand was fumbling at the vial for the blue pills. There was nothing to do now but wait—and, for her, waiting had never been easy.

Chapter 12

The priests had not been gentle. From where he stood Clarge could see the crusted blood marring Dumarest's left cheek, the ugly bruise on his right temple. Red welts showed at his throat and his lips were swollen. Injuries which could have been caused when he fell but which had more likely been given by those answering the alarm in the treasury. And there could be no doubt as to his bonds; thin ropes tied with brutal force clamped him to a thronelike chair. His boots gave his legs some protection but the flesh of his hands was puffed, purpled from the constriction at his wrists.

To the priest who had accompanied him Clarge said, "Bring water."

A table stood in one corner of the room. Clarge moved it, set it down before Dumarest. A chair followed and he sat, waiting, looking at the man for whom the Cyclan had searched for so long. One now trapped, helpless, hurt and suffering. The fantastic luck which had saved him so often before now finally spent.

"The High Priest has given me permission to question you. I trust that you will not be obdurate."

Dumarest made no answer. His head still swam a little from the effects of the gas and, like an animal, he had withdrawn into himself to escape the pain of his body, his bonds. Retreating into a private world in which he saw again the deep-set door which Chang had indicated. The door through which they should have passed to the inner chambers, the secrets they had come to find. To learn them, take what they could, to escape by the route the thief had prepared. A daring plan which could have worked. One ruined by the fighter's greed. Well, Sanchez would pay for it as would they all. Now it was each for himself with survival the golden prize.

He moved his head a little as the priest returned with the water, accentuating his weakness. But there was no pretense as to his thirst and he gulped the water Clarge held to his mouth.

"Is that better? Would you like more?" There was no charity in the cyber's offer—it would be inefficient to attempt to hold a conversation with a man unable to speak. "Here."

"Thank you." Dumarest breathed deep, inflating his lungs, striving to clear his senses. Here, now, would be his only chance of life. A wrong word, a wrong move and it would be lost. "I must congratulate you for having found me."

"It was a simple matter of logical deduction."

"Simple?" Dumarest shook his head. No cyber could feel physical pleasure but all shared the desire for mental achievement. It would do no harm to let the man bask in his success. "You have succeeded where others have failed."

As yet, but the real success still had to come. Clarge glanced at the priest. "That will be all. Withdraw now. Wait in the passage."

"The High Priest—"

"Ordered you to attend me. Must I report your disobedience?"

Dumarest waited, then as the door closed behind the priest he said, "I am in pain from my hands. Would you please loosen the bonds."

"There is no need."

"The pain makes it hard to think. Harder to remember."

"You know what I want?"

"Of course. Loosen the bonds and we'll talk about it." Dumarest looked down at his hands. "It would be better to cut the rope. Use my knife."

It was still in his boot—an apparent act of criminal stupidity on the part of the priests but Clarge knew better. The knife, Dumarest's clothing, the chronometer he wore, even the thin, black robe were, like himself, a violation of the Temple. Symbolic dirt to be kept together for united disposal.

Clarge pulled free the blade, ran the edge against the ropes, backed as they fell from Dumarest's arms. Placing the knife on the table he produced a laser from within his wide sleeve.

"Do anything foolish and I will use this. I will not kill you but—"

"I know." Dumarest stretched his arms and flexed his fingers, baring his teeth at the pain of returning circulation. He was still fastened by legs and body to the chair but something had been gained. "You'll burn my knees, char my elbows, sear the eyes from my head. I've heard it all before. Crippled I would still be of use to the Cyclan—but not this time. Or have you forgotten what they intend doing with me?"

Clarge had no doubt. Dumarest was to die—but when he died the precious secret would die with him. Escape was impossible and logic dictated the inevitable should be accepted.

"The affinity twin," said Dumarest. "The secret of how the fifteen biomolecular units should be assembled. You want me to tell you the correct sequence."

Fifteen units—the possible combinations ran into the millions. Since it had been stolen the laboratories of the Cyclan had been striving to rediscover it but time was against them. It took too long to assemble and test each combination. Eventually the secret would be found but it could take millennia before it would happen.

Clarge said, "Give me the secret and I will speak to the High Priest on your behalf. It may be possible to avoid your execution."

"I will be allowed to live?" Dumarest stared at the cyber. "What is your prediction as regards that probability? High or low? What are my chances?"

"I will do my best."

As he would butcher Dumarest cell by cell to get what he wanted. As he would tear and rend

his brain with electronic probes, to leave him a
thing of blind and mewling horror devoid of any
claim to humanity. Garbage to be seared to ash,
to be flushed away and forgotten once he had
yielded what he knew.

Dumarest lowered his face to conceal his eyes,
the raw hate he knew they must contain. The
Cyclan had cost him too much. Turning him into
a hunted creature forced to run, to hide, to forgo
happiness. To see those he loved destroyed before
his eyes. He had no cause to love the scarlet robe.

Yet the cyber was his only chance of life.

"The secret." Dumarest looked at his hands.
"I'll give it to you—but you must promise you'll
do your best to save me. You must swear to
that."

"You have my word."

One he would keep; the Cyclan did not deal in
lies. Clarge would speak to the High Priest but
what the outcome would be was immaterial. Once
he had the secret Dumarest would cease to be of
value. The cyber looked at him where he sat, a
man tense, afraid, advertising his fear. One willing to do anything in order to stay alive.

An impression Dumarest did his best to maintain. The cyber didn't know him; recognizing him
from a remembered description, accepting his own
admission of identity. Those who could have
warned him were dead, victims of their own false
assessment. Logic could, at times, turn into a
two-edged weapon.

Dumarest said, "A secret's no good to a dead
man. You can have it. Give me paper and a stylo
and I'll write it down."

He flexed his fingers and rubbed his hands together. It was inevitable they should have been freed—a man cannot write with his hands lashed fast.

"Here." He flipped the paper across the table with the tip of the stylo. "This is what you want."

Fifteen symbols scrawled in the order of correct assembly. Clarge studied them then looked at Dumarest.

"Write them again."

The second set matched the first and was just as worthless; a random pattern Dumarest had long since committed to memory. A possibility the cyber couldn't fail to consider. Had Dumarest, desperate to survive, set down the truth? Or was he being stubbornly uncooperative for the sake of some emotional whim?

"You don't trust me," said Dumarest. He was deceptively casual. "But I'll give you more. Help me and I'll give you all you could hope for. I'll give you the affinity twin!"

It rested in the hollow of the cyber's hand; two small ampoules each tipped with a hollow needle, one the color of a ruby, the other that of an emerald. Twin jewels but far more precious than any to be found in the entire universe. The secret for which the Cyclan had searched for so long.

The knife in which they had been housed lay to one side on the table, the pommel unscrewed and resting beside the blade, the hollow hilt now filled with nothing but shadows. A neat hiding place; the pommel had been held by an unbroken weld and Clarge had bruised his hands in the effort needed to break it. Now both knife and bruises were ignored as he looked at what lay in his palm.

The artificial symbiote which was the affinity twin.

Injected into the bloodstream it nestled at the base of the cortex and became intermeshed with the entire sensory and nervous system. The brain hosting the submissive half would become an extension of the dominant partner. Each move, all sensation, all tactile impressions and muscular determination would be instantly transmitted. The effect was to give the host containing the dominant half a new body. A bribe impossible to resist.

An old man could become young again, enjoying the senses of a virile healthy body. An aged crone could see her new beauty reflected in her mirror and in the eyes of her admirers. The hopelessly crippled and hideously diseased would be freed of the torment of their bodies, their minds given the freedom of uncontaminated flesh.

It would give the Cyclan the domination of the galaxy.

The mind and intelligence of a cyber would reside in the body of every ruler and person of power and influence. Those dominated would become marionettes moving to the dictates of their masters. Slaves such as had never before been known, acceptable façades for those who wore the scarlet robe.

"That's it," said Dumarest. "Now it's yours. I guess it will win you a rich reward."

The highest. Clarge would be elevated to stand

among those close to the Cyber Prime himself.
To direct and plan and manipulate the destiny of
worlds. To set his mark on the organization to
which he had dedicated his life and then, when
his body grew too old to function with optimum
efficiency, to have his living brain set among
those forming the heart of the Cyclan. To gain
near immortality.

And now he had regained the secret of the
affinity twin to spend the endless years in body
after body.

If he had regained it.

Clarge looked up from what he held in his
hand, seeing Dumarest seated before him, the
casual attitude he wore, the hint of a smile curving his lips. A man who had given in too quickly,
demanding nothing more than a bare promise to
help save his life. Odd conduct from someone who
had run so far, hidden so well, fought so stubbornly to retain what he had now so willingly
given.

Was he so fearful of death? If so why hadn't he
demanded stronger guarantees? Why had he so
meekly surrendered?

"Your prize," said Dumarest as again the cyber
looked at what he held in his hand. "I wish you
joy of it."

A jibe? Had there been mockery in his tone?
Those poisoned by emotional aberrations took a
distorted pleasure from illogical behavior. Was
Dumarest enjoying an anticipated revenge?

Clarge moved his eyes from the ampoules to
the papers, the symbols they bore. It was as easy
to write falsehood as truth—the information so

freely given could be worthless. The vials could contain nothing more than colored water. Was he the victim of a preconceived plan? Would Dumarest, even while dying, gloat over his victory?

"I say I wish you joy of it." Dumarest leaned back in his chair, now openly smiling. "I'm not being generous, cyber but, as I said, what good is a secret to a dead man? You don't really believe they will ever let you leave the Temple, do you?"

"They have no reason to prevent me."

"Since when has superstition had anything to do with reason? You know too much. You know where the Temple is and you have been within it. You know what lies inside. You have details of the treasury—they think I will have told you. Now, cyber, be logical—why should they let you stay alive?"

Logic and the acid test of reason. Clarge remembered the High Priest, the fanaticism dwelling in his eyes. A man, by his standards, hopelessly insane. One dedicated to the Temple and what it stood for. He had been adamant as to Dumarest's release, blind and deaf to the fortune offered for his unharmed body. Dumarest was to die as the others were to die and, in the end, Varne had lost his patience.

"You may talk to the man but that is all. You will be attended. The interview will be short. Do not ask again for his release. To do so would be to spit in the face of the Mother."

Would such a man fear the might of the Cyclan?

Clarge knew the answer—Varne wouldn't recognize any power but his own. Already he could be regretting having yielded to those who had arranged the interview. Torn with religious unease at the thought of having committed sacrilege.

Dumarest said, guessing his thoughts, "You'll be eliminated. Wiped out before you leave the Temple. You'll never even reach your raft. You have a raft?"

"I came in one. It was to have waited. The men escorting me are servants of the Temple."

"So you're alone. An easy victim. Who will miss you? Who can help?" Dumarest added, dryly, "You have the facts, cyber. Now extrapolate the probability of your leaving here alive."

Too low an order for comfort. Clarge looked at the papers, the ampoules in his hand. Dumarest's revenge: to give him what he could never use.

"I want to live," said Dumarest. "I assume you want to live also. Together we can manage it. There's a way it can be done. You have it in your hand."

"What?"

"The affinity twin." Dumarest was no longer casual, no longer smiling. He spoke hard, quickly, conscious of the passage of time. "Use it on the priest attending you. He will take over my body. Release it, change robes and put his own in the chair. He will be able to guide you from the Temple and take you to your raft."

"As you?"

"Yes. He will be confused but tell him he has been blessed by the Mother. Anything. Just get him to obey."

"And then?"

"I will be myself again when he dies. That must be arranged before you leave. He will be

unconscious, in an apparent coma. Open a vein
so that he will slowly bleed to death. That will
release me. I'll be alive, you'll have the secret
and we'll both be free." Dumarest glanced at his
chronometer. "But hurry. You'll only get the one
chance. Inject me now then get the priest after
you've called him in."

"Which is the dominant half?"

"What?" Dumarest's hesitation was barely noticeable. "The green one."

The truth, but Clarge didn't believe it. Already
he had assessed the potential danger of the plan;
should Dumarest take control he could kill, free
his body, carry it from the room and make his
own escape. It would be natural for him to lie
and the slight hesitation had betrayed him. The
liar's pause in which one answer was changed for
another. And another factor influenced his decision; red was the hue of power, of domination, of
the robe he wore. Red—the color of victory.

Transition was instantaneous. One second he
was sitting, bound and slumped in the chair, the
next he was standing, swaying a little, hands
lifting as he turned toward the cyber. Hands
which were not as he remembered, muscles not
as familiar. Instead of clamping on the cyber's
throat the fingers missed, tore at the robe, closed
on bone and sinew. Before Dumarest could shift
his grip Clarge was on the attack.

He twisted free, eyes betraying his belated recognition of the trick Dumarest had played. One
hand dived into his sleeve as Dumarest reached
for his throat, reappeared holding the laser as

the fingers tightened, fired before they could take his life.

A shot which would have killed had not Dumarest jerked aside his head, the beam ruining an eye and charring half his face. Dropping his hand he snatched at the weapon, twisted it as again it vented its shaft of destruction. Again it hit, lower this time, the muzzle aimed at the stomach, driving a charring beam into the intestines, searing the liver and creating a lethal wound.

Dying, Dumarest fought back, grinding the wrist he held, the weapon, turning it, thrusting the muzzle against the body of the cyber as he pressed on the finger riding the release. A moment and then suddenly it was over, the cyber's dead weight sagging against his body, the scarlet robe charred in the region over the heart.

As he fell Dumarest leaned on the table, gasping, fighting the waves of darkness which threatened to engulf him. The knife caught the sight of his remaining eye and he snatched up the blade, dropping to his knees beside the chair holding his limp body. Ropes parted beneath the edge and he slumped, hovering on the edge of darkness. An oblivion which could last too long— already the priests could be coming for him.

Turning the knife in his hand he drove the blade into his heart.

Dumarest rose from the chair, feeling the sweat dewing his face and body, the tension which knotted his stomach. To kill himself, even in a surrogate body, had not been easy. Stooping he pulled the knife from the dead priest's body, frowning at its feel, the loss of balance. Stability regained as he screwed back the pommel. Wiping the steel on the cyber's robe he thrust the knife into his boot then heaved the man into the chair at the end of the table. Quickly he stripped off his thin, plain robe, exchanged it for the blazoned one of the priest, lifted the man and set him into the throne-like chair. Ropes held him, the cowl masked the ruin of his face, the robe covered the blood from heart and stomach.

If anyone should look into the room they would see the cyber interrogating the prisoner, the priest in attendance standing by.

One armed with knife and laser—small weaponry to defeat the might of the Temple. And the pretense couldn't last for long. Dumarest cursed the cyber's too-quick recognition of the trap. He should be standing as the priest now with his own body wearing the scarlet robe cradled in his arms. He could have walked from the Temple to the raft and safety. A plan ruined by the cyber's belated realization that, to the vast majority of emotionally normal people, red is the color of danger.

Now he no longer wore the body of the priest. The robe with its red touches was stained with even more. To follow the original plan would be to invite death—there had to be another way.

He looked at the instrument on his wrist, pressed a stud, watched as the hands spun then came to rest. Up and toward the center of the Temple. The place where Altini would have made his opening and set the guiding beacon.

Dumarest remembered the treasury, the enigmatic door, the inner chambers which could con-

tain the information for which he had searched
so long. It could be lying waiting for him. Close.
So very close. Too close for him to walk away
now.

He had just one gamble, probably the greatest
risk he had ever been forced to take. Now he had
no choice but to follow his winning streak.

The passage outside was wide, flanked with
doors, the roof bright with illumination. Servitors moved slowly along busy with polishing
cloths, dusters, brooms. Two priests wearing the
sunburst insignia passed him without comment.
Another, wearing circles, glanced at Dumarest
and lifted a hand in an esoteric gesture. One
Dumarest returned far too late for it to have
been clearly noticed. The priest walked on un-
aware of how close he had been to death.

More servitors, a small group of women dressed
in ceremonial regalia, a priest wearing a robe
blazoned with a quartered circle who strode, head
bared, arrogance stamped on his thin features.

Dumarest hurried on, intent on a task of mo-
mentous importance. He reached a junction, chose
a path without hesitation, found what he was
looking for in a passage less brightly lit than the
other.

"You!" His finger stabbed at a priest wearing a
robe similar to his own. One with a face younger
than most and with an air of recently acquired
importance. "Accompany me to the treasury. Go
before."

In the Temple age carried seniority and the
snap of command induced the reaction of obedience. The priest looked at Dumarest, failed to see

the face masked by the cowl, took him for what he purported to be. Even so he had questions.

"The treasury? Is there trouble, master?"

"The violators. More has been learned. One has confessed to leaving an explosive device." Dumarest had no need to counterfeit urgency. "There is no time to waste. Hurry!"

He fell into step behind the other as the man led the way. A willing guide through a tortuous labyrinth in which Dumarest would have quickly been lost. As they reached a familiar area he slowed.

"This will do."

"You wanted my help."

"You have given it." Dumarest lifted his hand as if in blessing. "Remain here. Others will be following."

He moved on down the passage, to the wall where the carved beast crouched snarling, locked in stone. As before the passage beyond was empty. As he reached the room containing the cleaning materials he heard the pad of running feet. Turning he saw the priest running toward him. Recognized danger in his face.

"You are not of the Guardians!" The priest's voice held triumph. "I had my suspicions and now I am certain. Twice I led you wrong and neither time did you notice. And your robe is soiled."

"You fool," said Dumarest. "I gave you your chance."

"To wait while you violated the treasury? How many of you are there? Never mind, you will tell us—and then you will make reparation to the Mother."

He came in a rush, hands lifted, opened into blunted axes. A man trained in the skills of un-armed combat, using feet, knees, hands, elbows, the battering ram of his skull in order to gain victory. One with his mouth opened to scream a warning and summon aid.

Dumarest met the rush, blocking the slash of a hand with his forearm, sending the heel of his palm to slam against the other's jaw. A blow which did no real harm but delayed the warning shout. As the priest again opened his mouth Dumarest snatched at his knife and sent the pommel hard against the man's temple. A second blow and the fight was over, the priest slumped on the floor, unconscious, blood on the broken skin.

Laser in hand Dumarest ran to the far end of the passage, the lighted well, the sunken door. Like a shadow he passed through it into the area beyond.

Chapter 13

He had expected mystery, he found enchantment: a curving hall truncated at each end to form a segment, the outer wall rising up and sweeping over to meet a circular central area. The door through which he had passed gave on a narrow gallery which ran up and down the curving wall. Dumarest followed it down, seeing blazing words set into the stone; gold and silver polished to a mirror smoothness and forming abstract symbols, quartered circles, regimented quatrains.

The floor was of tessellated stone shaped in diamonds of red and grey. Scattered lanterns threw a diffused illumination, creating shadows in high places; pools of dimness touched by gleams of gems and precious metals. The place was almost deserted and he guessed it was a hall reserved for special ceremonies held at predetermined times when priests and priestesses would conduct ancient rituals.

He trod softly to the nearest wall, to a door set in an arch of stone. It gave on another chamber similar to the one he had just left but larger in that it encompassed more of the central area. The lighting here was brighter, the place crowded with robed figures, and Dumarest turned, hugging the wall, checking the instrument on his wrist.

It was getting close to dawn when the Temple would wake to thronging activity. The swinging hands pointed up and in as they had before, the angle steeper now. The beacon must be at the edge of the central dome which, he judged, topped the central area. To get into it, to climb, to find the opening and escape before the new day bathed the external area with light. To do all this and discover what he had come to find.

Dumarest scanned the walls, seeing the flare of gold and gems, the symbols now grown familiar, the marching quatrains. Philosophy repeated in every chamber, inscribed on every wall. Words which like the engraved flowers, the soaring birds, the fish and wide-eyed beasts touched with jewels and delineated with skins and feathers of laminated foil glowed like the denizens of paradise.

One which held a bloody fruit.

They hung at the far side of the chamber, arms lifted, wrists fastened to a ring which encompassed an upright pole. Men, stripped, bodies ugly with wounds, faces tormented with the agony inflicted on them. Nighted robes surrounded them as if they had been animals set out to feed predators and the faces turned toward them held expressions Dumarest had seen before. The gloating sadism, the blood-lust, the avid hunger of the degenerate to be found in every ring. But these were not watching men fight with naked steel but spectators reveling in the spectacle of pain. Of the agony of men impaled on cones of polished glass.

Dietz, Lauter, Sanchez.

But for the cyber he would have been among them. Would still be among them if he was caught.

Dumarest moved, edging to one side, careful not to attract attention. A man among others trying to get a better view. His lips moved in emulation of those around him as they droned invective. Shielded by his sleeve his hand clasped the laser as his eyes gauged angle and distance. One chance and if he failed he would be impaled with the others. But it was a chance he had to take.

He moved again, edging closer, working his way to the front of the crowd. Dietz hung, sagging in his chains, head slumped forward on his chest. The blood between his thighs was crusted and dark but there had been no time for his weight to have driven the pointed cone deep and he could well be still alive. As could Lauter despite his earlier wounds. There was no doubt about Sanchez. The fighter had a virile strength and an anger to match. Even as Dumarest edged into position, Sanchez lifted his head, eyes opening, mouth working to create a gobbet of spittle.

"To the Mother!" Deliberately he spat. "To the Great Whore of Creation!"

Dumarest surged forward with the rest, screaming his rage, taking his chance. The laser was a short-range weapon, silent, devoid of a guide beam, efficient only at close quarters. Sanchez slumped as it charred a hole in his heart. Lauter was next, an ooze of blood at his temple showing where the beam had hit. Dietz didn't move as Dumarest shot him in the throat, searing the carotids, releasing a turgid stream.

Death delivered with mercy—but there would be none to give him the same should he be caught.

Dumarest backed, the laser hidden, leaving the crowd as inconspicuously as he had joined it. Within seconds he was clear of the throng. A minute and he was again edging along the wall leading to the central area. An opening gaped in it, high, pointed, surmounted by a quartered circle shining with the gleam of polished gold. Two priests stood before it armed with heavy staves, weapons which clashed together to form a barrier as Dumarest approached.

"Halt! None may enter the Holy Place."

"My forgiveness but the insult done to the Mother—"

"They have paid and will continue to pay."

The robes concealed armor; Dumarest had caught the glint of metal beneath the fabric. Scales which would resist the beam of a laser, the thrust of a knife, and he guessed their faces would be also protected. He stepped closer, his hands lifted, open, obviously empty. A man apparently beside himself with rage.

"I must pay homage to the Mother. I—"

He stumbled and almost fell, lunging forward

to regain his balance, rising with the stave of the left-hand guard clutched in his hand. Holding it while the other became a fist which battered the robe, the flexible armor beneath, driving both fabric and metal against the man's throat. As he fell, gasping, spitting blood, Dumarest tore free his stave and sent the end like a spear into the other's cowl. Bone snapped and blood gushed from the shattered nose. A second thrust and the man had joined his companion on the floor.

Dumarest jumped over them, reached the opening, ran through it and up the stairs which wound in a tight spiral beyond.

They led to the Holy Place.

There was magic in it; the emanations of generations of worshipers who had taken stone and metal and created a thing greater than the components which had gone into its making. A sacred place, one set apart, a small area which held the condensation of belief. Here, for those who worshipped, was reality. Here the naked, undeniable truth. Here, if anywhere, would be what he had come to find.

Dumarest stepped from the opening at the top of the stairs, head tilted, eyes wide as he surveyed what lay before him.

A circular chamber topped by a dome the whole filled with a misty blue luminescence which softened detail and gave the illusion of vastness. One dominated by the figure which occupied the center. The statue of a woman, seated, her head bent as she stared at her cupped hands, the ball which hovered above them.

The Mother. The sacred image of the Temple—it could only be that. A woman with a soft, grave face, hair which rested in thick coils about her head and shoulders. The gown was plain, full-skirted, the type often favored by those wedded to the land. Her hips and breasts were swelling curves of fecundity. Her eyes held sorrow.

Dumarest stepped closer to where it stood. The statue was, he judged, about twelve times life-sized, the cupped hands some seven feet across. They, the entire statue, the stool on which it sat, was carved from some fine-grained stone the dull brown material unrelieved by any adornment or decoration. The ball hanging above the cupped palms was about ten feet across and he studied it, frowning, wondering as to its purpose, the markings blotching the shining, metallic surface. A ball poised before her, one she had just tossed upward or was about to catch. Or was it something more than that? The symbolism had to be important. A ball—or was it representative of something special? A world, perhaps?

A world!

Earth!

It had to be Earth!

Dumarest felt a rising tide of excitement as he studied it, the deep-cut markings marring its surface, the irregular shapes, the huge triangular continental masses. The Earth, he was certain of it. The Earth and the Earth Mother—there had to be more.

He turned, eyes searching the interior of the chamber. It was set with fluted columns which rose to converge like the interlocking fingers of mighty hands across the sweep of the dome. They matched the wall itself in its gray, metallic dullness. One broken at points with figures incised in gold.

Dumarest stared at them, at the dark mouths of openings giving on to the chamber. Some must lead to stairs such as he had climbed, others held the glint of crystal. All could soon vent a stream of guards. He could guess what would happen to him should he be caught.

He looked at his wrist and touched the stud of the instrument strapped there. The hands now signaled a point almost directly overhead. He threw back his head, eyes narrowed as he searched for the opening which was his only hope of survival. A flicker of movement caught his eye, another. Altini, crouched on a ledge which ran around the lower edge of the dome, gesturing with searing urgency.

"Earl!" His voice ran in echoes around the chamber before dying in fading murmurs. "Earl! Up here, man! Hurry!

Dumarest ran for the wall as sounds came from beyond the openings. Men, marshaled by priests, preparing to rush. A threat which gave strength to his hands, cunning to his feet. The fluted column held roughness and he found it, used it to climb like a spider over metal which crumbled in places beneath his fingers.

"You made it!" Altini sucked in his breath as Dumarest joined him. He was sweating, his skin unnaturally pale. "Get anything?"

"No."

"Me neither. There's damn all down there worth

the carrying." The thief gestured toward the statue, the misted chamber. "So much for Ishikari and his promises. The thing's a bust. What about the others?"

"We got caught. Gassed and taken. I was lucky. They weren't."

"How lucky?"

"A cyber arrived. He wanted to know things and chose me to provide the answers. He's dead now. Like the others."

"Dead? But how? I saw them. I'd set the beacon and was widening the hole when I heard voices. Chanting and such so I froze. Some priests came in and had the others with them. There was talk about homage being paid to the Mother and some other stuff then the priests left. There was a blue glow. I saw something like it earlier when I acted the pilgrim but this was different. It made the air taste peculiar. Afterwards I did some thinking. Then I took some action. Those bastards won't play any more games in the name of holiness."

"Tell me."

"Never mind." Altini shifted on his ledge and Dumarest saw the direction of his eyes. "You'll know all about it when it happens. How did the others die?" He blinked as Dumarest told him, looked at the laser in his hand. "Neat, clean, but it took guts. I'm glad you did it. I liked Kroy a lot and being stuck on a cone is no way to die. The bastards! But they'll pay!"

"How?" Dumarest was sharp. "What have you done? Tell me, damn you! Tell me!"

"That ball." Altini pointed. "They lower it and

it glows. It's hung from the dome, see?" Again he pointed. "Well, I've fixed thermite charges to the rod. Acid detonators. When they go the rod'll fuse and part. The ball will fall. The glow will start and they'll be too worried about it to think of us. Neat, huh?"

A man clever in his trade but with limitations. Altini could pick a lock, a pocket, rob a safe, break into a guarded place, steal without leaving a trace. But he had never acted as crew on a vessel, knew nothing of physics, was ignorant as to the workings of power plants and atomic piles. Dumarest looked at the suspended ball, the hands cupped beneath which now, he could see, held the same metallic shine as the globe. Metal set within the stone, blocks fashioned to follow the curve of the ball.

He remembered the workers, their sores, their emaciation.

Karlene's dreadful fear which caused her to wake screaming in the night.

"Out!" Dumarest rose to his knees on the ledge. "We've got to get out! Now!"

"Earl—"

"Out, damn you! Out!"

He thrust the thief before him to where a narrow opening gaped just beneath the lower edge of the dome. One cut on the slant to block the passage of light. Altini reached it, twisted so as to enter it feet first, looked to where he had been before.

"It won't be long now, Earl. If—"

"Move! Damn you, move!"

Dumarest turned as the thief obeyed, looking

again at the statue, the ball, the golden figures incised on the walls. Finally at the slender rod almost invisible against its background of matching color. The charges Altini had set made a swollen protrusion. Even as he watched, smoke seemed to rise like the plume of smoldering incense.

"Earl? I'm clear."

Dumarest dived into the opening, head first, wriggling, clawing his way past the riven stone. Cooler air touched his face and, with another twist, he was free, rolling down a slope, checked by Altini's hand.

"Steady." The thief's voice was a whisper. "Take it slow and careful. There are alarms, watchers—"

"We've no time." Dumarest rose to his feet, laser in hand. "Run for it."

"But—"

"Run!"

He set the lead, racing over the roof, the slope adding to his speed. A wire caught his ankle and he stumbled, falling as a man called out and the shaft of a guide beam seared the air where his head had been. Light accompanied by energy which cracked stone and left a glowing, vivid patch. As Altini rolled past him, Dumarest turned, firing, his own weapon making no betraying signal. Doing no damage either and he wasted no more time. Escape lay only in speed, the deceiving glow of starlight, the slowness of the guard's reactions. By the time they had spotted the flitting shadows, aimed their weapons, their target had vanished.

Dumarest fell again as he neared the edge,

something moving beneath his boot, and he rolled, catching vainly at the eave, missing to plummet down to the ground below. Luck was with him; the wall which could have broken his spine brushed his shoulder, the stone which could have smashed a knee or his skull rested an inch from his face when he hit the dirt.

"The raft!" Dumarest sprang to his feet as Altini landed beside him. "Where did you leave the raft?"

"To the west." The thief made a vague gesture. "Slow down, Earl. They'll forget us soon. They'll have something else to worry about."

"Keep moving!" Dumarest saw a shadow thicken on the summit of a wall, fired, saw stars gleam where the darkness had been. Stars which were beginning to pale. "There's another raft. The one the cyber came in."

"I saw it. Over at the main entrance."

"Let's get it!"

Altini led the way, slipping along in shadow, reaching walls, climbing them to drop on the far side. Cautious progress and far too slow. Dumarest forged ahead, ran along narrow ledges of stone, jumping, racing, taking chances as savage fingers of destruction reached toward him. Seared plastic stung his nostrils with acrid stench and hair flared over the wound on his scalp. Fire quenched by his own blood. The thief wasn't as lucky.

Dumarest heard his scream, saw the guard standing to one side, weapon lifted to send another blast of fire into the twitching body. A man who shrieked as invisible death burned the sight from his eyes, the life from his brain.

"Ahmed?" Dumarest knelt beside the thief. "Bad?"

"In the guts." Altini writhed on the dirt, face silvered by the starlight. "Don't waste time." He beat at the hand Dumarest extended toward him. "This is no time to go soft. Take your chance— but leave me the laser."

He screamed as Dumarest raced on; the sound of an animal at bay, trapped, hurt, defying those who hunted him down. Deliberate noise which attracted attention, targets for his laser, as he provided a target in turn. Dumarest reached the last wall, sprang over it, crouched in the shadow at the far side. Luck was with him, the raft stood to one side of the great doors, the two men in attendance looking to where the thief had died.

The first fell beneath the hammer-blow of the pommel of Dumarest's knife. The second fell back, one hand lifted to the gaping slash in his throat, the other raised in futile defense. The body of the raft was empty. Dumarest threw himself at the controls, forcing himself to take his time, not to overload the initial power-surge. As men came running toward him the vehicle lifted, darted higher as he fed power to the generator and the antigrave units, which gave it lift.

From below a laser reached toward him and solid missiles from a tower chewed at the rail. He ignored both weapons, concentrating on height and speed, sending the raft hurtling toward the west.

Higher. Higher. Reaching toward the stars ur ·

til sanity checked him and he dived, riding low, dropping beneath the peaks of hills, following valleys, keeping rock and stone between himself and the Temple.

Flinging himself down into the body of the vehicle as, with shocking abruptness, the night vanished to reveal the terrain with ghastly clarity. Stroboscopic brilliance streaming from behind where a sunburst flowered to create a searing mushroom against the sky.

"A bomb," said Rauch Ishikari. "An atomic bomb. I find it hard to believe."

He sat in the salon of the *Argonne,* his clothing disheveled, his face bearing the marks of tension and strain. He looked older than he had, robbed of sleep, the culmination of a dream. As he reached for the decanter to pour wine, his hand shook a little so that thin, delicate chimings rose from the contact of container and glass.

"It's true enough." Dumarest leaned back in his chair. His throat was sore from explanations and his body ached from Ellen Contera's administrations. Drugs and other things to treat his wounds and wash the absorbed radiation from flesh, blood and bone. "It's what you wanted to find out. The secret of the Temple. The object of their veneration. I wish I could give you more but Sanchez—"

"Sanchez was a fool! One blinded by greed. I should have recognized his weakness—such men are never to be trusted." Ishikari gulped at his wine. "But a bomb? They worshiped a bomb?"

"They worshiped the Mother," corrected Dumarest. "The Earth Mother. The statue and the bomb were symbols and they may not have known it was a bomb at all. Once, maybe, but they could have forgotten. It had become a part of their ceremonies; the depiction of Earth cradled in the hands of the Mother. Both were radioactive substances which neared critical mass when brought close. When that happened there would be an intense blue glow."

"Radiation," said Ishikari. "Altini saw it."

And had seen it again without the protection of reflective surfaces. Dumarest wondered if the thief had guessed he was dying—that his body was doomed to rot just as those of the workers were rotting. Contaminated as the priests who had attended the Holy Place had been contaminated. Experiencing the affliction which had cursed a world.

Dumarest looked at the wine and saw in the ruby liquid images of an ancient horror. A planet riven with suicidal madness. One shunned, proscribed, set apart by those fearful of the contagion of insanity. One forgotten. A world deliberately lost.

Earth.

It had to be Earth.

"It's gone." Ishikari shook his head radiating his disappointment. "Everything I'd hoped to find. Now there's nothing left but a crater filled with radioactive slag."

"You blame me?"

"No, of course not."

But he would be blamed, Dumarest knew, if not now then in a week, a month, a year. When

Ishikari had brooded long enough over the votive offerings now lost, the books, the gems, the cunning artifacts. The history which the Temple must have contained. The secret knowledge which he would be certain had been there to find. The power he yearned to obtain.

By that time they would have parted—already the *Argonne* was heading to a nearby world. One where he could take a choice of vessels.

Leaving the salon Dumarest made his way down the passage. Ellen was within her cabin, wine at her side, a plate of small cakes resting beside her on the bed. She smiled as he knocked and entered; then reached for the bottle, halting the movement of her hand as he shook his head.

"No? Well, you know best. I thought you could use it. I guess Rauch has pretty well sucked you dry."

"There wasn't that much to tell."

"I agree—if you told me all there was."

"You doubt it?"

"Does it matter?" Shrugging, she held onto the bottle and filled her glass to the brim. "Some secrets should remain just that—secrets. You know what I'm doing?"

"I think so. You're holding a wake." He saw she didn't understand. "A party to say farewell to the dead."

"You'd know about such things. Just like Kroy. He told me how mercenaries operate. How to stop your enemies haunting you and how to settle with your friends. The few I had are still around. I was too close to them for too long. Help me, Earl. What should I do?"

He reached for the bottle and filled an empty glass and lifted a cake from the plate at her side.

"You do as I do. You sip and take a small bite and eat and swallow and take another sip. Each time you do it you say farewell." To Kroy and Ahmed and Pinal the assassin. To Ramon Sanchez and the man he had killed. Watching the woman, counting, Dumarest wondered why she had included him also. A man she had never seen and could know nothing about. Who else had died? "Where is Karlene?"

"Earl—"

"Take me to her!"

She lay on her bed like a woman carved from alabaster, white, pristine, pure, with the face of a child. She lay on her side, knees drawn up to her chest in the fetal position, one hand at her mouth, the lips closed around her thumb. Her eyes were open, wide, as vacuous as the windows of a deserted house.

"Karlene?" Dumarest stepped toward her. "Karlene?"

"It's no good, Earl." Ellen drew him back as the woman made no response. "She can't hear you. She's locked in a world of her own. Her talent drove her to it."

"The Temple?"

"It dominated her when young and stayed with her all her life. She knew what was going to happen. She *knew* it! It kept coming closer and in the end she had to run from it. But it was always there and Rauch, the fool, had to bring her back. She couldn't rest. All the time you were away I kept her under sedation but it wasn't enough.

When the Temple blew—Earl, can you guess how she must have felt?"

An entire community of men and women—how many he could only guess. All dying in a furious blast of ravening energy, seared, blinded, torn, broken—death had been fast but thought would have been faster. Each victim would have had a fraction of time to know the shock and fear of extinction.

The scent which had blasted Karlene's mind.

"She could only escape into the past," explained Ellen. "But, for her, the past was never a happy time. So she kept regressing until she went back into the womb. Catatonia. I may be able to do something with her eventually but she'll never be the woman you remember."

Another ghost to add to the rest. One who had smiled and held out her arms and embraced him with a fierce and demanding passion. A woman who had led him to the place where he had found the secret for which he had searched for so long.

The golden figures incised on the grey, metallic walls of the Holy Place.

Figures which he knew beyond question were the coordinates of Earth.

Soon, now, he would be home.

DAW

Unforgettable science fiction
by DAW's own stars!

E.C. TUBB

☐ SYMBOL OF TERRA   UE1955—$2.50
☐ ANGADO   UE1908—$2.50

M. A. FOSTER

☐ THE WARRIORS OF DAWN   UE1994—$2.95
☐ THE GAMEPLAYERS OF ZAN   UE1993—$3.95
☐ THE MORPHODITE   UE2017—$2.95
☐ THE DAY OF THE KLESH   UE2016—$2.95

C.J. CHERRYH

☐ 40,000 IN GEHENNA   UE1952—$3.50
☐ DOWNBELOW STATION   UE1987—$3.50
☐ CHANUR'S VENTURE   UE1989—$2.95

JOHN BRUNNER

☐ TIMESCOOP   UE1966—$2.50
☐ THE JAGGED ORBIT   UE1917—$2.95

ROBERT TREBOR

☐ AN XT CALLED STANLEY   UE1865—$2.50

JOHN STEAKLEY

☐ ARMOR   UE1979—$3.95

JO CLAYTON

☐ THE SNARES OF IBEX   UE1974—$2.75
☐ A BAIT OF DREAMS   UE2001—$3.50

NEW AMERICAN LIBRARY
P.O. Box 999, Bergenfield, New Jersey 07621

Please send me the DAW Books I have checked above. I am enclosing
$_____ (check or money order—no currency or C.O.D.'s).
Please include the list price plus $1.00 per order to cover handling
costs.

Name _____

Address _____

City _____ State _____ Zip Code _____
Please allow at least 4 weeks for delivery

DAW

DAW BRINGS YOU THESE BESTSELLERS BY
MARION ZIMMER BRADLEY